W9-AHL-719

"THIS IS NO EASY ASSIGNMENT.

Chandler is tough. A man breaks the law, and if he gets away with it, it does something to his ego. He gets to believing he can't be stopped. It's time to knock some of the fat out of these hardheads down there. It's apparent the local people can't do it. That reckless streak of the men crowding into Chandler has to be curbed completely. Think you can handle it?"

Bud's eyes shone. "I can sure take a whack at it."

THIEVES' BRAND

Giles A. Lutz

BALLANTINE BOOKS • NEW YORK

Copyright © 1981 by Giles A. Lutz

All rights reserved. Published in the United States by Ballantine
Books, a division of Random House, Inc., New York, and si-
multaneously in Canada by Random House of Canada, Limited,
Toronto, Canada.

Library of Congress Catalog Card Number: 80-2905

ISBN: 0-345-30254-0

This edition published by arrangement with Doubleday & Com-
pany, Inc.

Manufactured in the United States of America

First Ballantine Books Edition: June 1982

Chapter 1

Bud Carson was a newcomer to Chandler, Oklahoma, and it showed. He didn't have the positive mannerisms of a man who felt he belonged here, and that reflected in the fixed frown on his face. He hadn't worn the deputy marshal badge long, and he had been in town even a shorter time. He had spent many an hour thinking about it. Perhaps his newness was too apparent, but this was like everything else: a man had to earn his niche, regardless of where he was or what he was doing.

Bud was a tall, lanky man with alert gray eyes. His face now was too somber, but now and then a smile chased that forboding appearance away, turning his expression warm and friendly. So far, however, he hadn't found many things to smile about in this rough, new town. There wasn't a timorous bone in his body, and to the casual observer there seemed to be no shrinking in him. Perhaps that insecure feeling would vanish when he firmly established himself.

Chandler was a young and growing town, but its roots seemed anchored in pure deviltry. With each passing week, its reputation for toughness and pure cussedness had grown. It had increased to such an extent that reports had reached the ears of higher authority in Oklahoma.

Bud would never forget the day Marshal Nix called him

into his office. Nix was mad! His eyes burned, and his jaw was set.

"Chandler's at it again," Nix said in a clipped voice. "They shot down another sheriff. That's the sixth in the last four months. The mayor is frantic about the situation. He wrote that the town is completely out of hand. No man is willing to pin on the sheriff's badge. He's asking for help."

Bud scowled at him. "You mean six sheriffs have been cut down there?"

Nix shook his head. "No, three quit and handed in their badges. The other three were gunned down. It amounts to about the same thing."

He leaned back in his chair. Long years of dedicated, hard work had built up his reputation as the premier law officer in Oklahoma. Bud had never heard how many men Nix had shot in the pursuit of his duty, and Nix would never talk about it. He had been up against some of the most infamous outlaws in the annals of crime, and the fact that he was still in office spoke well of his ability.

But the long years were beginning to show in the lined face and the slumping shoulders. He didn't move as sprightly as he once had, and a long chase after a wanted man left him dragged out for days afterward. Bud wondered how much longer Nix would remain in his position. Nix was up against something no man could ever whip—the encroaching years. No matter how renowned a man's record was, there came a day when he was simply too old. It could happen to Nix, too, as it happened to every man.

Bud was grateful that his father had worked with Nix for a half-dozen years a long time ago. Bud didn't remember his mother too well. She died when he was only four, but he grew to adore his father. Emory Carson had left law work and settled on a small farm outside of Guthrie. He had worked at it as hard as he had in earning his badge, and he was slowly making a success of the farm when he had a tragic accident with a runaway team. Bud found him in the smashed wagon, and the memory of that awful moment would never leave him.

He didn't remember the funeral too well. He had gone

through the following agonized days in a numbed daze. It took two weeks to get his brain working again, and the solution to his delemma came all at once. He didn't want to remain on the farm—not that he couldn't run it, but the place held too many memories. Every way he turned, he would see some reminder of his dad. He couldn't take very much of that.

But the solution was right before his eys. He had never met Marshal Nix, but his father had talked of him often. The association between his father and Nix gave Bud an in. If Nix had an opening, he would hire him.

Nix had looked up as Bud entered the office. He stared long at Bud, then exclaimed, "I'll be damned, Emory's boy."

"How'd you know?" Bud asked. He hadn't said a word.

Nix grinned. "You're the spitting image of Emory. What brings you down this way?"

That terrible hollow hit Bud in the stomach again. He sat down uninvited, afraid his legs wouldn't support him. "Emory was killed in an accident a little over a month ago," he said bleakly.

The shock of the announcement showed on Nix's face. For a moment it was blank, then it set in stern, unyielding lines. "No," he protested, "damn it, no. How did it happen?"

Bud briefly recounted the episode of the runaway team. "Pa didn't get out of the wreckage."

Nix kept shaking his head as though he could erase the words by refuting them. "I can't believe it," he muttered. "Emory was one of the best men I ever worked with. Lord, the close scrapes he's been through, then something as ordinary as a runaway team carries him away." He looked at the frozen agony on Bud's face and said, "I guess you don't want to talk about it."

Bud nodded, his lips clamped in a tight line. He felt the moisture in the corner of his eyes. A moment more of this, and he would lose control.

"Sure, sure," Nix said, in instant understanding. "What can I do for you, Bud?"

"I'd like a job, if you have one open," Bud replied.

"Emory taught me how to use a gun. I think I'm qualified."

Nix nodded. "If Emory taught you, that's enough recommendation for me. How soon can you go to work?"

"Today," Bud returned.

"I need someone. You're hired," Nix replied. "Hang around Guthrie for a while. It'll give you the feel of the job."

That had been two months ago. Bud had learned a little about his job, though it didn't fill the void in his life. He had hoped for something more demanding, and this strolling about Guthrie's streets hadn't begun to answer that demand. Then Nix had called him into the office.

"Something just came up, Bud. It might be asking too much of you, but you might as well get your feet wet."

Bud waited impatiently for Nix to go on. He didn't care how tough the assignment was; he could erase some of the doubts in Nix's mind by showing his ability to handle any job.

"Go on," he said tersely.

Nix leaned back and laced his fingers behind his head. "Bud, I'm sending you to Chandler. That town started out tough and is daily growing tougher. We kept waiting for the local law to handle the situation." He shrugged, and that wry gesture told of how the local law had failed. "It just didn't happen. I guess the men the local voters elected had been around the lawbreakers too long. Seeing their depredations for so long filled them with fear. I just heard that the mayor of Chandler can't even find a man who wants to challenge any of those hooligans. He's begging this office to send him help."

Bud's eyes gleamed. "Are you sending me?"

"Does that bother you?"

Bud thought he caught a challenge in Nix's voice. He shook his head. "I was wondering when I'd start doing something to earn my pay."

A warm grin spread over Nix's face. "Thought you'd feel that way. But I've got to warn you, Bud, this is no easy assignment. Chandler is tough. A man breaks the law, and if he gets away with it, it does something to his ego.

He gets to believing he can't be stopped. It's time to knock some of the fat out of those hard heads down there. It's apparent the local people can't do it. That reckless streak of the men crowding into Chandler has to be curbed completely. Think you can handle it?"

Bud's eyes shone even brighter. "I can sure take a whack at it."

"Don't go down there thinking it's going to be easy. If Emory taught you to use a gun, he taught you right. That's why I'm overlooking your youth. If it's necessary to use a gun to enforce your authority, don't hesitate." He grinned bleakly. "I know the class of men you'll be going up against. There's nothing that can make them swallow harder than a few dead men. It seems to jerk them up short and makes them think."

He squinted at Bud. "Does this kind of talk worry you?"

"When I hired on, I knew I wouldn't be teaching Sunday school."

Nix shook his head, and there was admiration in the gesture. "That's what I wanted to hear. That bunch in Chandler has to be taught that the law applies to everybody. It looks as though only a hard lesson can do it. I'm handing you a tough job, Bud. But remember this: A few dead men builds up a man's reputation."

"I never shot a man," Bud said, his voice not quite steady. It rankled him to think Nix had some doubts about him. He was only twenty-two years old, but he knew what to expect when he asked Nix for the job.

Nix chuckled frostily at the heated color washing Bud's face. "My sentiments exactly," he said softly, "or I wouldn't have picked you to go down there. I just wanted to be sure you know what you could be facing."

"I know," Bud said flatly. He stood and rolled his shoulders to ease the ache in them.

He hadn't reached the front door when Nix stopped him. "Bud," he called. "If things get too sticky, you know where to turn for help."

A sheepish grin stole across Bud's face. "I do. I'll try not to need any help."

"That's what bothers me," Nix said. "That you won't admit even to yourself that maybe you've bit off more than you can chew."

Bud's grin spread until his whole face was aglow. "If I'm that stupid, then I'll deserve whatever happens. I've been watching a man who's pretty good at his job. I've learned something."

"I think you have," Nix said simply. "Good luck, Bud."

Chapter 2

Chandler was too new to have railroad facilities. Bud had to take a stage for the last lap of the journey. Four other passengers were in the stage, and Bud caught their curiosity as they looked at his badge. There might have been some hostility in that surveillance, and Bud stared back at them until they looked away uneasily. Were these citizens of Chandler returning from some trip, or just passing through town? If they were in the first category, it wouldn't take long for the news of the arrival of a marshal to spread. The marshal's purpose? That was easy. Bud speculated on how it would set with the gentry that had been terrorizing Chandler, then closed his mind to such thinking. He would find out soon enough.

He waited until the others stepped down from the stage, then collected his valise and took the long step to the ground. Chandler wasn't an impressing town. Its business district might run two blocks, but that would be giving the town the best of it. Bud would say maybe a hundred houses made up the rest of the community. Their newness was evident in the raw lumber used in the structures. A few houses had been painted, but by far the majority had that gleaming yellow of lumber not up long enough to be seasoned. Another year and that yellow would have faded into a uniform gray.

Bud glanced down the street. Five saloon signs stuck

7

out over the walkway. That was quite a few for a town this small. The competition for business would be severe, and Bud wondered how they managed to survive.

He glanced up, and the driver was watching him curiously. Bud grinned and said, "Not much of a town, is it?"

The driver soberly shook his head. "Don't let the townspeople hear you say that. They're kind of touchy about the town they're building. In less than a year's time, the town has doubled in size."

Bud nodded in agreement. He could see a half-dozen structures under construction. At the end of the business district he could see the larger buildings of new businesses. Yes, Chandler was growing. If the lawless element could be curbed, this town might thrive enough to make its mark.

"I'll remember that," Bud said quietly.

The driver nodded in return and whipped up his teams.

Bud remained motionless until the stage disappeared from sight. Oklahoma's familiar red dust settled slowly around him, and he coughed at its acrid bite. He spat to rid his mouth of the taste, but that didn't completely do it. He decided he'd better have a beer. One saloon was as good as another, and he headed for the nearest one.

He felt a tingling, electric warning run across his skin the moment he stepped through the door. It was too quiet, and that ominous silence carried its warning. Bud's gaze went warily over the room. There were at least a dozen customers here, and that seemed too many for this time of day.

Every eye in the room was fastened on him, but each time Bud looked at a man they shifted uneasily away. Only one man boldly met his eyes, a big burly redheaded man. Even motionless he seemed to have a swagger in his posture. That warning was now clanging in Bud's head. If trouble started here, it would come from this man. Finally, Bud looked away and walked up to the bar.

Something unusual caught his eye. A woman attended the bar, and he had never looked at a more handsome female. She was tall, carrying her shoulders with a regal dignity. Her hair was jet black, flowing over her shoulders in silky waves. The light wasn't good, but what there was of it played in that shining mane, raising sparkling highlights all over it. Her black eyes were almond shaped and slightly upturned at the corners. Her nose was a beautiful line, and the full mouth was on the petulant side.

Bud found himself breathing harder. This woman was a looker. He had known a few women in the short period of his life when he became aware of the opposite sex, but nothing like this one. He was hit hard. His heart was accelerating to the beat that literally shook him, and his hands were sweating. He wondered what she was doing behind that bar. Probably filling in for the regular bartender while he took a short break.

"Howdy, ma'am," Bud said with a broad smile. He judged her to be older than he, and as yet unattached, for he saw no ring on her left hand. The age didn't make any difference.

She didn't respond to his smile. If anything, her eyes seemed to grow more frozen. "What do you want, mister?"

Hearing her voice was a small shock. It was almost harsh with a nasal twang to it. Bud didn't let his disappointment show. The unattractive voice was the only flaw he could see in her.

"Make it a beer, ma'am."

She nodded indifferently and walked a few paces to draw a schooner.

Bud couldn't take his eyes off her. Lord, she moved with a grace that was as fluid as flowing water.

She drew a beer, and his eyes clouded. Half of that schooner was foam. She hadn't worked long as a bartender, or she didn't give a damn. Bud didn't protest. He wasn't going to be at cross purposes with her over a poorly drawn beer.

She served the beer sloppily, slamming the schooner down before him. Beer splashed all over the bar, and she didn't apologize. In fact, that might be a challenge in those hard eyes, as though she might be daring him to protest.

"Thank you, ma'am," Bud murmured. He met her eyes

squarely, and she looked away. He chuckled inwardly. For
the first time, she noticed him as an individual.

"Good beer," he said, sipping at his mug. She tossed her
head half-angrily, picked up a bar cloth, and cleaned up
the mess she had made.

Bud kept his face sober, though he wanted to laugh
aloud. It looked as though he might be getting under that
tough defense.

She finished wiping the bar and cast him an angry
glance. But there was puzzlement there, too. She looked as
though she had run across something she couldn't quite
figure out.

Bud raised the glass to his lips again, and a voice said,
"I figured you were too young to drink a man's drink." It
was a positive tone, its overtones grating to the ear.

Bud slowly turned his head, and he looked at the redheaded man. The man's face was aglow with an evil
pleasure. He had moved out a couple of feet from the bar
and was squarely planted there.

"What drink is that?" Bud asked mildly.

The redhead slapped his thigh. "Did you hear that,
boys? The new marshal is in a saloon, and he doesn't
even know what a man's drink is."

Bud slowly turned until he faced the redhead. This man
intended pushing this confrontation until he had a seething
pot of trouble. Bud couldn't guess what his purpose was,
but it came as a bad smell from the man.

"Why, damn it," the man roared, "it's whiskey."

"That so?" Bud didn't raise his voice. "Right now, I prefer beer."

The redhead's intentions were now plain. His head was
pulled down into his shoulders, and his lips were slightly
parted as though he tasted something good.

"What if I tell you beer's an offense to good drinking
men?" the redhead purred.

Bud was aware of every movement in the room. Men
had instinctively pulled away from the troublemaker. They
smelled something evil, too.

"That's telling him, Lem," one of them chortled.

Their manner and expression told Bud he was all alone

in this room. The woman was watching all this, but Bud didn't dare turn his head to catch her expression. If there was a protest in her at this brewing trouble, she didn't express it.

"That's tough," Bud said coldly. "Right now, I still prefer beer."

That took Lem aback, and his mouth went slack. He gulped, and his lips clamped together. He might be a little surprised at Bud's acceptance of his interruption, but he had no intention of backing up.

"Who in the hell do you think you are to talk to me like that?" he roared. "Or maybe you think that piece of tin on your vest protects you?"

"Don't push it any further," Bud warned. "I was minding my own business."

"Listen to him," Lem said. His voice hadn't lowered. "He *does* think that piece of tin is protecting him."

Bud drew a deep sigh. "I suggest you do the same thing," Bud said frozenly. He remembered Emory's advice: *"I hope you never get into a spot where you have to use your gun. But if it happens, keep your attention riveted on your opponent's eyes, not his hand. The eyes will give away his intentions."*

Bud never looked away from Lem's eyes. They were angry right now, but they weren't burning with a special purpose. "You'd be smart to take my suggestion," he said firmly.

Angry color filled Lem's face. "Get out of here before I throw you out!" he roared.

That drew a collective gasp from the watchers. They pulled back even farther, leaving a wider swath around the two. Evidently, Lem wasn't used to having people cross him.

"I'll give you ten seconds to get out of here," Lem panted.

Bud smiled slowly. "You're wasting your breath." The words were soft and spaced.

Lem recoiled as though he had been slapped. "You can't talk to me like that." His words were choked, and he had trouble getting them out.

"I just did," Bud taunted.

That tore away the last restraint. Evil purpose was naked in Lem's eyes, making them blaze.

Bud waited no longer. He had no doubt this man was fast. He wouldn't dare to be so aggressive if he wasn't. Bud's hand dropped to his gun butt. He didn't have to recollect what Emory had taught him. It had been pounded into his head so hard that the words were engraved there. All he had to do was open the doors to that teaching and let it take over. He had never faced a man in a gun fight, and he would always wonder just how good he was until the moment came.

Bud's draw was smooth and unflawed. He had already decided what his target would be. The head was too small; the torso presented a much better one. He aimed at the spot where the ribs reached an apex. He didn't actually watch Lem's draw, but he was aware that the man was fast. Bud pulled the trigger and felt the kick back of the gun. Then he heard the second shot. It came only a split second later. But Lem had already been hit, and he was doubling over as he pulled the trigger. He grunted harshly as the bullet struck home, and there was surprise and agony in the sound. His bullet buried itself in the floor a short distance from Bud's feet.

Bud watched him closely. From somewhere Lem might find enough vitality to try another shot. The hand holding the gun was struggling with a tremendous weight. Sweat broke out on Lem's face as he tried to force the hand to answer his will. The hand raised an inch or two, and Bud was ready to fire again. Then Lem's face contorted with a vicious wash of pain and the hand fell limply at his side. He was dead, then, though a reflex action gave a moment's semblance of life: his head came up, and he stared at Bud with surprise that plainly showed. Blood stained his lower face and shirt. His gun clattered to the floor, its thud making a distinct sound in the stilled room.

The release of tension in the room was a collective sound, like a small wind soughing through the trees. Bud looked around, his eyes cold. "Any of you want to pick this up?"

He got no response. He glanced at the blood on the floor. There must be a lot of blood in a man's body, for Lem had bled a large pool. Bud jerked his eyes away. This was the first time he had ever shot a man, and it left a sickening taste in his mouth. His stomach rolled, and he thought he was going to be sick.

He put the gun away and turned back toward the bar. "Sorry for all this mess, ma'am," he apologized. "I want to finish my beer now."

She looked directly at him, and there was new warmth in her eyes. She saw him as an individual, not a faceless blob. "It wasn't your fault," she said. "Lem has always been a troublemaker. He pushed you into doing what you did."

Bud's smile was strained. At least she wasn't blaming him, and that was a small consolation. He took a sip of his beer, and it tasted flat and brackish.

She read the distaste in his grimace and extended a hand. "Give me your mug. I'll refill it for you."

Right now, he didn't want any more beer, but he couldn't refuse it. She was trying to be considerate. Refusing her might be as jolting as a slap in the face.

She came back with the mug, and Bud noticed she had used more care in drawing this one. The foam was at a reasonable level, and she didn't splash it all over the bar.

He nodded and said, "Thanks. I'll get someone to help me carry him out."

She stared directly at Bud, and there was respect in her eyes. "I never thought I'd see that happen. Lem was good with a gun."

Bud smiled faintly. "Then I can consider myself lucky."

She shook her head in sudden exasperation. "Don't take it so lightly, mister. I'm telling you he was good."

Bud's face was completely sober. "I know that. He came close to getting that shot off." That streak in her was decidedly unfeminine. She had seen a man killed, and she could talk calmly about it. He wouldn't say it had destroyed his interest in her, but he would approach her with a different viewpoint.

He couldn't get all the beer down, and he set the half-finished schooner on the bar. He reached in his vest pocket for a coin to pay for it, and she shook her head as he laid it on the bar.

"That one was on the house," she murmured.

"Thanks," he replied. The beer wasn't setting well on his stomach. He had better get out of there before his weakness disgraced him.

"Where can I find Mayor Ira Crump?" he asked. "He's expecting me."

Her eyes sparked with interest, but she didn't comment. "He owns that little white frame house at the end of the street."

"Thanks again," he said and touched the brim of his hat. "I'll see you again?"

"Maybe," she said indifferently.

He didn't look back from the door, though he wanted to. Her indifference had thoroughly dampened his interest. That was going to be one tough woman to know, but he still intended to try. The silence still held in this room, but what had happened here would keep tongues wagging for days to come. He half wished he could hear what would be said. Particularly, he would like to know what went through that woman's mind.

Chapter 3

Bud found the small white frame house with no effort. The only thing outstanding about it was that a fairly new coat of paint made it stand out among the houses around it.

He knocked on the door, and a querulous voice called, "Who is it?"

"I'm deputy marshal Bud Carson. Marshal Nix sent me down to talk to you."

The door opened, and a man below average height stood there. Only a fringe of white hair surrounded the bald pate, and Bud knew a disappointment at the sight of him. This harassed man didn't seem capable of running a town no matter how small it was. The shoulders were slumped, and the face was deeply lined, the lines of worry and care. Bud couldn't see anything that could have persuaded the voters to put this man into such a position of responsibility. He didn't appear capable of handling the ordinary chores of daily life, let alone the burden of guiding the affairs of a town.

"Marshall Nix said you needed help."

Those tired eyes stared at him in open disfavor. Bud didn't miss the tightening in them as they swept over the badge pinned on his vest. Crump didn't like what he saw either.

"I made it plain to Marshal Nix that this town had gotten completely out of hand. I didn't expect him to send someone so young."

That thrust didn't reach Bud. Rarely had he seen a job where age was the one prerequisite. The only measurement that was important was could the man do the job.

"I think I can handle it, sir," he said easily.

"You don't know what's been happening here," Crump said waspishly. "I've had three sheriffs killed on the job. Three more just simply handed back their badges. They didn't say so, but their quitting admitted they couldn't handle the job."

Bud's jaw hardened. This old man could be hardheaded and set in his ways. "When I stepped off the stage, I walked into a saloon for a beer to wash the dust out of my mouth. One of the customers made some remarks about my drinking beer. I told him to drop it, but he wouldn't listen. He kept badgering me until I couldn't take any more. He got what he wanted from the first—a gun fight. You know, I think the badge bothered him more than my drinking beer."

A drastic change came over Crump. He stood a little straighter, and the weariness seemed to drop from him. A spark fired his eyes, and he asked, "Did you know the man?"

Bud shook his head. "Never saw him before. He was a big, redheaded man. I heard one of the men he'd been drinking with call him Lem. Do you know him?"

"Hell yes," Crump yelled. "Lem Mallory. He's been the cause of most of the trouble around here. He killed two of those sheriffs. It got so that everybody was afraid to look cross-eyed at him. I sure ain't sorry to hear he's gone."

"You think that'll ease some of your trouble?"

"I doubt it," Crump muttered. "It may lose some of its force. Mallory was the ringleader of the crowd that persisted in breaking the law. But his dying won't stop the trouble." He looked at Bud with worried eyes. "He's got two brothers. One younger, one older."

Bud shrugged. "Those kind usually do."

"Don't take them too lightly," Crump warned. "They

aren't as good with a gun as Lem, but they'll gang up on you. You'll have to watch out for both of them."

Nix had given Bud a rough assignment. It had started out raw and violent almost from the first moment he set foot in this town.

"Just don't get careless," Crump said.

"I don't intend to," Bud said easily. "If something happens to the remaining Mallorys, will that stop the trouble?"

Crump pursed his lips in thought, then shook his head. "I doubt it, but it'll put the brakes on it. The Mallorys were the ringleaders. They issued all the orders, and nobody dared question them. If the law can put halters on them, I think the followers will back up. At least, they'll be doing some blinking before they look again. I'm worried about you."

Bud chuckled. "Why?" Only a few moments ago, Crump had thought him too young to handle this job.

Crump had the grace to color. "I know how I acted," he admitted. "I thought you were far too young. I see I was wrong. Now, I'm just grateful Chandler has you." A tremulous smile moved his lips. "Forgiven?"

Bud laughed. "For what? You didn't do me any harm. There's something else I want to talk to you about."

"Anything you want."

"There was a good-looking woman behind the bar." Bud described her briefly, drawing on the vivid picture of her engraved on his mind. "She served me, but I didn't get her name. What was she doing, substituting for somebody?"

That tickled Crump, and he cackled until he was breathless. "Substituting, hell. She owns that saloon."

Bud blinked in surprise. "That's an odd occupation for a woman."

"She's been around a saloon ever since she could toddle. Her mother died when she was just a baby. Her father was Hank Jenkins. Lilah got used to being around a saloon. She grew up living above one. She got her experience early. She was serving the bar before she was fifteen."

That explained a lot of things. Bud thought of the hard mask on that lovely face. That was probably in self-defense, a method of warding off the more impulsive customers. Bud couldn't blame her for whatever she used to keep too attentive males at bay.

"It must have been a rough life for her," he mused.

"She can handle it."

Bud glanced at Crump in surprise, for the voice was venomous. Crump caught the judging and bristled. "I ain't making a surface judgment. A lot of funny things have come out of that saloon."

Bud was getting annoyed with this crotchety old man. "Such as what?" he challenged. His tone said, if you're accusing her, you'd better be able to back it up.

Crump knew that what he said had offended Bud. "I got eyes. I've been around Chandler long enough to observe what's going on."

"You still haven't named anything specific," Bud said frozenly.

"Old Hank got in several scrapes with the law. A bad class of people frequented his saloon. A couple of times, Hank was charged with horse stealing."

"Was it ever proven?" Bud snapped.

"Those two charges weren't. But the horse stealing didn't stop, either. The law was ready to charge him again when Hank died. He left the saloon to Lilah."

"That was the natural thing to do," Bud said in disgust. "Because a girl has to make her living the best way she can, people judge her. Particularly when she's a handsome woman."

Crump squinted at him, an obscene mirth in his eyes. "I can see you're taken in already."

That stung Bud. Crump was implying his judgment wasn't good. "I've also seen where an old man's judgment is warped."

That put Crump to spluttering. "Damn it, I know what I see."

"You still haven't pointed out anything," Bud observed.

"The same class of people still frequent the saloon," Crump howled. "You ran across Lem Mallory in there, didn't you?"

Bud got control of his tongue. "The saloon was open to anybody."

Crump glared at him, his eyes narrowed and hot. "You young ones never learn anything. The female of the species is the deadlier."

"What's that supposed to mean?" Bud asked hotly.

"I'm telling you meanness could run in the family. I'm trying to tell you to keep your eyes open. Maybe you'll see what I'm talking about."

"I'll do just that," Bud snapped. He had started out so well. His shooting of Mallory had solidified his place with the mayor of Chandler. Now all that was wiped out. He didn't like that, but he'd be damned if he'd let Crump prejudice him.

He started for the door, then stopped. "Do I have an office here?" Maybe Crump wouldn't want him in town. He waited for a response.

Crump stared at the floor. "The sheriff's old office is at the end of the business district. I'm afraid it pretty dirty. It hasn't been occupied for almost a month."

"It'll do," Bud said coldly.

He started to turn again, and Crump stopped him. "I hoped we could work together."

Bud spun to face him. "We can, if you don't try to tell me how to run my life."

Crump's face reddened. "I'll never bring it up again. I've told you. If that doesn't open your eyes, then I can't do anything more."

Bud could feel the heat of rising rage in his cheeks. He wasn't going to get along with this old man, not unless he agreed with everything Crump said.

Crump's anger was building again. "When it comes to hardheadedness, there's nothing like a young pup."

Bud glared at him. "I came down by stage," he said, trying to keep his voice reasonable. "I'll need a horse to get around. Can you recommend a good place to buy one?"

"Sam Little runs the only livery stable in town. Watch him if you try to deal with him. He's slicker than fresh ice."

"I can take care of myself," Bud growled. He left without another word. He walked down the street, his boot heels coming down hard. If this wasn't a miserable start. Nix had sent him down here, and in a way he was only responsible to Nix. But Crump was the mayor. He should make some attempt to get along with him. Did Crump have enough power to send him packing? That was something to think about.

Bud found the livery stable at the edge of town. It wasn't an imposing place, but in the big corral outside of the stable there were six horses. Bud stood at the fence looking them over. He prided himself on his horseman's eye. He should be able to find what he wanted out of those six, if they were for sale.

His presence disturbed the horses, and they raced around the corral, a big palomino in the van. He was a flashy animal and carried his head high.

The horses made four complete rounds of the corral. Bud watched them with a practiced eye. At first judgment, he would pick the palomino, but something intangible bothered him. Did he hear something in the horse's breathing? He thought he did, a wheezing, distressed sound. The palomino could be wind broken.

The horse in the rear was a hand shorter in height. He was ugly and didn't carry his hammerhead high. But his head was thrust belligerently forward, and he was trying to make up the distance between him and the palomino. His coat was dull and his tail was on the scrawny side, but there was something that reached out to Bud. This was one of those rare horses that came along once in a man's life. This horse was a stayer, and no matter how far he was outdistanced, he would keep on trying.

The longer Bud watched the horses, the more convinced he was he wouldn't choose the palomino.

"What do you think of them?"

The voice startled Bud, and he glanced at the kid who had moved up beside him so noiselessly that Bud hadn't heard.

The speaker was just a kid. Bud doubted that he could be fifteen, but he was well grown for his years. By the time he had finished growing, he would be a good-sized man. His hands were big and ungainly, and he seemed to stick out at every joint.

He was sloe eyed, and a lock of tow hair straggled over one eye. "Do you like them?"

"Maybe," Bud answered cautiously. "Do you know anything about them?"

"I should. I work for ol' Little."

"Which one do you like?"

"Not the palomino. He's been wind broken. Little has been trying to move him."

"But you wouldn't buy him?"

The kid's snort was an eloquent answer. "You feel the same way," the kid observed.

"I didn't say that," Bud corrected him. "But if I had to pick one, it'd be that little hammerhead."

The kid nodded approvingly. "You got a good eye, mister. He can go all day and half of the night. You won't go wrong on him." The boy extended his hand. "My name is Billy Campbell."

It was said with such simplicity that it was appealing. The growing-up years were the nice ones.

"I'm Bud Carson. The new marshal."

Billy cocked an eye at him. "I've heard about you. You've already made a big splash."

Bud winced. News got around too fast in a small town. Billy had already heard about the killing of Lem Mallory.

"I didn't want to do that, Billy," he said gravely.

Billy shrugged. "You couldn't do it any other way, could you?"

Bud liked this kid. He was making it easy for him. He started to answer when an outraged voice yelled, "Billy, what the hell are you doing out here?"

"I was just helping the marshal make up his mind about these horses."

The speaker came up to them, his face indignant. He was sloppy fat, and his belly wobbled as he walked. He wasn't too clean, and he hadn't shaved for three or four days.

Bud looked at him with disfavor. He didn't like a dirty

man, and he didn't like an adult who used his advantage of age over a kid.

"He was," Bud said coldly. "Are you Sam Little?"

The belligerence faded from the man's face. "I am, Marshal." There was a subtle fawning in his voice. "What can I do for you?"

"I want to buy a horse."

"You came to the right place," Little answered. He didn't actually rub his hands together, but he gave the impression. "Which one do you like? I can recommend the palomino. At the price I'm asking he's a steal."

"How much do you want for him?"

"Three hundred dollars. I bet you never thought you could pick him up that cheap."

"A little steep for me," Bud said. He had enough experience doing business with a horse trader to know not to accept their first price. He glanced at Billy, and the kid was determinedly shaking his head.

Little looked around in time to catch the gesture. "What the hell you shaking your head for?" he bellowed.

"A gnat was bothering me," Billy said defensively.

"You get inside and get back to work," Little roared. "I'll bet you ain't done half of your work today."

Billy started off, his face flushing. That calling down before another adult had stung.

"He seems like a good kid to me," Bud observed.

"He ain't worth a damn," Little said furiously. "I have to be on his tail all the time to get anything out of him." he saw the displeasure on Bud's face and said hastily, "To get back to the palomino."

"Too much," Bud said decisively.

He started away, and Little waddled after him. "Don't be in such a hurry, Marshal," he wheedled. "I see you've got a sharp eye. I'll knock twenty-five dollars off him, though I'll be robbing myself."

Bud shook off the pudgy hand and continued walking.

Little hastened his steps to catch up with Bud. "I'll make it fifty dollars," he begged, "though that's cutting my own throat."

Bud stopped and whirled to face Little. "I'll give you

seventy-five dollars for the little hammerhead. That's my only offer."

"Oh, God," Little wailed. "You're robbing me."

Bud grinned. "I'm not holding a gun on you." He turned and took a step.

Little moved to catch up with him. "All right," he moaned, "he's yours."

Bud chuckled and walked back with Little to the corral.

Little said mournfully, "Don't come back complaining to me if something goes wrong."

Bud grinned. "I promise you I won't. You got a saddle to go with him?"

Little's eyes turned crafty, and Bud guessed at what was running through his mind. Here was a chance for him to make up some of his loss.

He led Bud into the tack room and displayed three saddles. Two of them were hopeless wrecks, the third would do.

"I'll give you ten dollars for the good one, if you throw in a bridle and saddle blanket."

Little seized his head in both hands and rocked it back and forth. "Somebody should be arresting you," he said pitiously.

"I don't want the horse," Bud said firmly.

"You can't do that," Little wailed. "You made a deal."

"But I didn't pay you any money. I can find a horse someplace else."

"Take him," Little screamed. "The saddle, bridle and blanket are yours for what you offered."

Billy walked by at that moment, and Little vented his fury on him. "What did you tell him?" he asked in an ugly voice.

"I just told him the palomino was wind broke."

Little's face turned purple, and Bud thought he was going to have a stroke.

"You're always poking your big nose into business that doesn't concern you," Little wheezed. "You're fired. I don't want a kid like you working around my place."

"I don't care," Billy said with a show of a kid's bravado. "I could never satisfy you. It was a rotten job, any-way."

Little started to rush at him, his face twisted in an insane mask.

"Hold it," Bud ordered. "You haven't finished your business with me."

Billy darted to a safe distance, then stopped to thumb his nose at Little.

Bud looked at the purplish cast flooding Little's face, then said, "Better get out of here, Billy. Meet me at the old sheriff's office."

"Sure," Billy replied and walked away.

"Worthless, little smart aleck," Little grumbled. "It's plain to see he ain't had no training. How could you expect him to grow up to be an honest, law-abiding man?"

Bud finished counting money into Little's hand. "You know," he said reflectively. "He'll probably have a better chance than most adults." He winked at Little and left him sputtering.

Chapter 4

Billy was sitting on the step before the office when Bud rode up. He sprang to his feet, eyes glowing at the sight of the horse Bud had bought.

"You bought him," he exclaimed, his voice shaking with enthusiasm. "I was afraid Little would talk you into the other one."

Bud swung down and smiled. "You didn't have much faith in me," he reproved.

"That Little is a slick one," Billy said. "I've heard him tongue whip people before." His face clouded at some recollection. "I'm glad I'm not working for him anymore."

Bud shook his head. "I'm sorry you lost your job, Billy."

"It wasn't your fault. It's been a long time coming. I guess he was in a particularly bad mood today." He shrugged. "It doesn't matter. I couldn't satisfy him anyway."

But it did matter. Bud saw the clouds in the kid's eyes. It may not have been much of a job, but it was valuable to him.

Bud peered into the window, but it was too grimy and fly-specked for him to make out much of the office's interior. Oh well, he could inspect it more closely. Crump had given him a key.

He unlocked the door, and the hinges squawked their protest.

Billy was at his elbow, and his mind was still on the horse Bud had purchased. "Have you thought of a name for him yet?"

"I think I'll call him Lucky."

Billy's eyebrows rose. "Why Lucky?"

"Because he gave me the chance to meet you."

That pleased Billy, and he flushed. He looked around the room and said, "Not much of a place, is it? Might do for pigs."

Bud could agree with Billy's judgment. It looked as though it hadn't been occupied for a year, not a month. Only one desk and chair made up the furniture, and inch-thick dust was over everything. "We're going to change all this," Bud announced.

"We?" Billy's voice was surprised.

"You're looking for a job, aren't you? You've got one. You're working with me to clean up this place."

Billy's face remained blank, and Bud knew a disappointment. "You don't like that kind of work?"

"I did worse for Little," Billy said slowly. "How do you know you want to hire me? You don't know anything about me. I might steal you blind."

Bud chortled at the idea. "What would you steal in here? Do you want the job or not?" Billy had said Little paid him fifty cents a day. Bud could do better than that. "I'll give you half more than Little gave you," he said.

Billy was still slow in accepting, and it annoyed Bud. "The pay offer isn't enough?"

Billy shook his head. "It's not that. You're the one who shot Lem Mallory." His face twisted ferociously. "I wish I could've seen it."

"You're pretty young to be so bloodthirsty."

"Nobody liked him," Billy said passionately. "He had a streak of meanness a yard wide. He used to come into the livery stable. Complained about everything I did for him." He stopped, and his eyes were far away, lost in some thought.

"What is it now?" Bud asked impatiently.

"I was just speculating on how long you'll last here. This is a rough town. Somebody will be coming after you."

Bud chuckled. The kid had a good head on him, and he used it. "I'll be around for a good while, and don't you forget it. Now make up your mind. Do you want the job or not?"

Billy's eyes weighed Bud figuratively. "I think you'll be around a good while, too," he said. "I want the job."

"Fine," Bud approved.

"Where do we start? This place is sure a mess, ain't it? Every time a sheriff was killed or turned back his badge, Mayor Crump had to get a poorer type. The good men saw what was going on and wouldn't have the job."

Bud laughed in delight. "I don't consider myself good, but I took the job."

"Aw, you're different. You're from out of town. You didn't know any better. I'm kinda worried about you."

Bud's eyebrows rose. "How's that?"

"I like you, and if you're hiring me, I want you to stay around a long time. Lem has two brothers, one older, one younger—both of them almost as mean as he was. They ain't gonna let this pass. They'll come looking for you." He hesitated as though pondering how to ask this awkward question. "Are you good enough to handle both of them?"

"Billy, I don't know," Bud answered soberly. "Two men are always harder to handle than one."

Billy bobbed his head. "That's what I figured. You better not let them have the first crack at you."

Bud suddenly felt a menace loom up. He hadn't the slightest idea of what the Mallory brothers looked like. "Have you seen them, Billy?"

"Lots of times. One of them is bigger than Lem, the other smaller."

"That's not much of a description. Anything that stands out about them?"

Billy's face screwed up with his effort to think. "Hell,

they're just ordinary looking. I can't think of anything that would pick them out."

"Are they redheaded like Lem?"

"They're sort of reddish haired," Billy said doubtfully. "But not flaming like Lem was."

Bud frowned. He must be on guard from two men without the slightest idea of what they looked like. He could bet they would know him. Then his face cleared as an idea struck him. "Billy, that's why I want you to go to work for me. When you see those two, you can point them out." There was still doubt in Billy's face, and Bud said as a clincher, "You said you wanted me to be around a good while. You could insure that."

"Well, I like you, and you outsmarted that old Little." Billy looked around the room again. "And I need a job." He grinned at Bud. "Looks like you've hired a boy."

Bud squeezed his hand. "Man," he corrected He'd rather have this kid working for him than aimlessly wandering the streets. "I can't pin a deputy badge on you, Billy. But it'd kinda be like it."

Billy's eyes glowed. "Say, that sounds good. It'd kinda be like doing law work, wouldn't it?"

"It would," Bud said gravely. "You'd rather be on the law's side than on the side of people like Lem, wouldn't you?"

"I sure would," Billy replied. "What do we do to start cleaning up this place?"

"Pick just about any spot you want. It needs it all over. The windows need washing, the floor needs sweeping, the walls could stand a good scrubbing down. Then maybe we'll give them a new coat of paint."

"Boy, you really lay out a list, don't you?"

"Don't you like work, Billy?"

"I'm a good worker," Billy answered, in quick defense. "It's just that everything you name is woman's work."

Bud shook his head. "You're putting the same tag on this work that most of the world does—either this or that is man's or woman's work. That's not so. If it's honest work and needs doing, it doesn't make any difference whether a man or a woman does it."

Billy gave that some thought. "That makes sense to me. What do you want me to do first?"

"Go to the hardware store and buy a couple of pails, two brooms, a mop, and some rags. Maybe later I'll send you after paint brushes and paint. We'll see."

Billy nodded, his eyes wide. "That's going to cost some money. Who's going to pay for it?"

Bud reached into his pocket and pulled our four dollars. "That ought to cover it. I'm going to try to convince Mayor Crump that the town should pay for it."

Billy hooted. "Nobody's been able to get money out of that skinflint. If you get him to pay for it, I'll tip my hat to you."

Bud chuckled, turned and pushed Billy toward the door. "You buy careful. What's left out of that money will be yours for the first day's pay."

Billy whooped and broke into a run. Bud grinned. There went one smart, observant kid. Could he tell him anything about Lilah? He scowled and shook his head. He wasn't going to use Billy to poke and pry deeper into Lilah's past just because an old man tried to instill suspicion of her in his head.

Bud used his handkerchief to wipe off the desk and chair. He sat down and rummaged through the desk drawers. He finally found a few faded sheets of paper in a bottom drawer. He pulled out one of them and found a pencil in the top drawer. It was dull, and Bud pulled out a pocket knife and opened a blade. When the pencil was sharp enough to suit him, he made a list of the things he had sent Billy to buy. He listed Billy's salary as four dollars and fifty cents a week.

Billy came back with his arms burdened with purchases. "I jawed old man Cummings down," he crowed. He pulled a dollar and forty cents out of his pocket and laid it on the desk before Bud. "I even got him to give us a bunch of rags without charge."

"Good going," Bud approved. He shoved the dollar and forty cents back toward Billy. "I told you what you saved would be your first day's salary."

"All right!" Billy said enthusiastically. "Where do I start?"

"First sweep the floor. Sweep it out of the door. After it's clean, it could stand a mopping."

He had never seen a kid work with more zeal. He picked up one of the buckets and asked, "Where can I get some water?"

"There's a public pump a block down the street." Billy was whistling as Bud went out of the door.

Bud filled his bucket, then looked at it doubtfully. Water alone wouldn't clean those grimy windows. Cummings' General Store was right across the street, and Bud walked into it, carrying his bucket of water.

Cummings was a merry-faced man. Bud judged him to be past his sixties. "You trying to sell me a bucket of water, Marshal? I can get all I want free." He chuckled at his little joke.

"I'm trying to clean some windows," Bud explained. "I hoped you'd have something to spark up this water."

Cummings walked to the end of a double row of shelves and came back carrying a bottle.

"It's not very big," Bud said dubiously.

"No, but it's powerful. You get a noseful of this stuff, and it'll rip off the top of your head."

Bud looked at the bottle with more respect. "How much do I put in?"

"Never used it myself," the store owner said and grinned. "Why don't you try putting in a little and see if it cuts the dirt."

Bud paid him a quarter for the ammonia. "I should have thought of that myself." He smiled at this cheerful little cuss.

"You come back if it don't work, Marshal. We'll see if we can figure out something else."

Bud picked up his pail of water. "I'll do that."

He carried the bucket and his purchase back to the office. Billy was just sweeping the last of the dirt out of the front door.

"How's it look?" the kid asked.

Bud looked at the floor. It was better but still far from clean. "I guess you're going to have to mop it."

"I was planning on that," Billy said and picked up the other pail and headed for the pump.

Bud splashed a little of the ammonia into the pail of water. He got a whiff of the stuff and recoiled, his eyes burning, his nose stinging. Cummings' comment was an understatement when he said this stuff was powerful.

Bud doused a rag into the mixture and stirred it thoroughly. He squeezed out the rag, keeping his head averted from that irritating smell. He made a tentative swipe at the big front window and felt like whooping as he saw the grime dissolve before the mixture. Cummings was sure right when he recommended ammonia.

It took a lot of rags to dry the washed part of the window. He had to go over the moistened, cleaned spot time after time. But if he kept at it, it was going to work.

Billy came in, carrying a pail of water. He looked at the window and said, "God Almighty. I wouldn't have believed it. You can see out of it now."

"Do you want to take this over, Billy? I'll get on the floor." At Billy's cheerful acquiescence he warned, "Just don't breathe too close to this stuff."

Uneasiness touched Billy's face. "Is it poison?"

"No, but it'll sting your nose and make your eyes water."

Bud carried the second pail of water to the back of the room so he could work toward the door. He looked doubtfully at the plain water. Maybe he should have gotten soap of some kind to mix with it.

He started mopping, using sheer muscle to cut through the dried mud on the floor. He could do it all right, but it was going to take a lot of pails of water, and his back would be aching before he was through.

He looked up as Billy broke into expletives that were startling coming from a kid.

Billy looked at him with smarting eyes. "You didn't warn me enough," he complained. "I got a good whiff of this stuff."

"You all right, Billy?"

Billy shook his head with such vigor that Bud was afraid it would fly off. "I'll be all right when my eyes stop burning."

After a moment, he went back to his window washing. Bud noticed he kept his face carefully averted from the pail.

At the end of the day, their struggles against the collective dirt and grim were showing progress. The windows were clean and sparkling, and even a good housekeeper would have been proud of the floors.

Billy sat on the corner of the desk, while Bud sank into the chair. "Would you say this is like house cleaning, Marshal?"

Bud nodded, wondering what Billy had in mind.

Billy stretched out his arms and flexed his fingers. "I never gave a woman enough credit for cleaning a house. Believe me, from now on it'll be different."

Bud grinned. Billy had a trick of going straight to the heart of a matter. "Women don't get nearly the credit they deserve," he said sagely.

"Yep," Billy said, staring straight ahead. "I guess if I live long enough, I'll get a little smart."

Bud chuckled. "As long as you can see that, there's hope for you."

"What do we do tomorrow, Bud?"

"We haven't even started on the walls"—Bud glanced up—"or thought about the ceiling. It looks like it's been walked on for years."

Billy sighed. "Seems like it never ends."

"You know today may have started making good husband material out of you."

Billy colored, and he growled. "That's the farthest thing from my mind. How about you? You ain't married yet, are you?"

"Not yet," Bud answered. "But I'm thinking more about it all the time. I guess I'm closer to the marrying age than you are." The picture of Lilah flashed into his mind. He wouldn't say he had already made his choice, but if it rested on her, he wouldn't have made a bad pick.

They walked to the door together, and Bud said, "See you in the morning. I've got to stop by and see Crump. I want to let him know what we've been doing."

Billy grinned impishly at him. "You hope to get your money back?"

"Something like that," Bud admitted. "You think I'm going to have trouble, huh?"

Billy cocked his head at him. "If you don't you'll be the first one. Good night, Marshal."

Bud watched Billy until the gathering dusk swallowed him. It was worth seventy-five cents a day just to have him around.

He knocked on Crump's door, and the mayor opened it. His face wasn't friendly. Evidently the argument of this morning still stuck in his craw.

"What is it this time?" Crump growled.

"That office was a pigpen," Bud said flatly. "I sure as hell didn't want to work in it."

"Clean it up then," Crump said acidly. He started to close the door.

Bud shoved the door back. "I've started cleaning it up," he snapped. He pulled the folded piece of paper from his vest pocket. "Here's what I spent for cleaning items."

Crump had to hold the piece of paper close to his eyes. When he looked at Bud, they were wild.

"Do you expect me to pay for all this?"

"I expect the town to," Bud said calmly.

Crump looked back at Bud's listing. "What's this seventy-five cents a day for?"

"I hired a boy to help me with the cleaning." Bud had to keep a stiff curb on his rising temper.

"I'm not paying it," Crump howled.

"That what I wanted to find out," Bud said coldly. "You didn't need help very badly, did you?"

That bald head was thrust at Bud. "What's that supposed to mean?"

"It means you're going to have to start all over looking for a law officer. I'm leaving. How long do you think it will take the roughnecks to find they can trample all over this town again?"

"You can't leave," Crump protested. "When I tell Marshal Nix about you deserting your post, he'll have your hide!"

Bud grinned wickedly. "When he learns what a cheapskate I was working for, he'll congratulate me for quitting."

He turned to go, and Crump bounded after him. He seized Bud's arm and begged, "Can't we talk this over?"

"I only talk to reasonable men."

"I'm reasonable," Crump implored. "Try me and see."

"How about the bill I gave you?"

Crump looked at the itemized bill again, and his face was sour. "Ordinarily it would have to go through the council, but because it's you, I'm paying it now."

He was true to his word. He paid the bill exactly, having to search the house for the last two pennies.

"What about the kid? How long can I keep him on?"

Crump gagged. "You think he's necessary?"

"He's necessary."

"I guess you can keep him on." Crump sounded as though the words were literally dragged out of him. He stabbed a bony finger at Bud. "But the minute you don't need him anymore, you let him go. I won't pay for any unnecessary help. Do you understand that?"

Bud kept his face straight. "Agreed," he said solemnly. "Now, one other thing."

He wanted to grin as he saw Crump tighten, bracing himself for another outrageous demand.

"What's the best boardinghouse in town? One that serves good meals?"

Crump let a breath of relief whoosh out. This new marshal couldn't expect him to pay for that. "Mrs. Edison. She runs a clean house, and she's a top cook. She was widowed three years ago, and she set out to support herself. Every report says she's doing an excellent job."

"Thank you, Mayor." Bud kept his face straight. "I think we're going to get along just fine."

He turned and walked away, looking back as he

reached the walk. He couldn't be sure whether Crump wanted him to quit or stay on. He laughed to himself all the way to the Edison boardinghouse. He wished Billy had been there to see that clash of wills.

Chapter 5

Bud belched contentedly as he left Mrs. Edison's supper table. The woman was an outstanding cook, and she served with a lavish hand. Bud patted his belly. He would have to be sure that he didn't let those generous meals run away with him.

He walked slowly down the street, speculating on how he was going to spend the evening. A lonely night in a boardinghouse, no matter how much he approved of what he had seen, wasn't much of a way to spend time.

Lilah's saloon was just a block ahead, and Bud's breathing increased. He couldn't ask for a better way to spend the remainder of the evening.

He quickened his pace and stepped into the saloon. It was filled tonight. He was noticed the moment he entered. He didn't miss all the side glances thrown his way. These men remembered him from last time all right, but he wanted to be accepted on more friendly terms.

Lilah could feel the same way as her customers, he thought as he approached the bar. She looked up as he neared, and there was no lightening of her features. He didn't exactly see rejection in her eyes, but he didn't see a welcome, either.

"Hello," he said tentatively.

She nodded indifferently. "What'll it be tonight? Beer?"

He could take a little satisfaction from the fact that she

remembered what he had ordered the last time he was in here.

"That'll do just fine," he said softly.

Bud watched her draw the beer. He was making some time with her, for she took more care in drawing the drink. She didn't let the foam build up, and she didn't spill any of the brew as she set it carefully before him.

"Thanks," he said, lifting the glass to her.

"For what?" she asked, in surprise.

"For remembering how I like my beer served."

He was rewarded with a flush, and she looked away quickly. Ah, he thought gleefully. He had made an impression upon her.

She took her time before she looked at him again. That was typically female; she wouldn't let him think she was too eager to solidify their acquaintance.

She mopped the bar before she spoke. "You made a lot of talk in here today."

"I did?" Bud feigned surprise. "How?"

"You know how," she said with a degree of annoyance. "Don't play stupid with me. You did it by shooting Lem." She jerked her head toward the other customers. "They're still talking about it tonight."

"Oh that," he said. He saw the annoyance increasing in her eyes. This was a different woman than most he had known. She wanted things honest and direct. She would never simper, and she never would be coy.

Bud changed his mental approach to her. "He asked for it. You saw it. I tried to avoid the fight, but he kept pushing."

She gave him a slight nod. "Yes," she agreed. "He certainly asked for it."

Bud thought the annoyance in her eyes had faded.

"Did you know who he was?" she asked.

"Not until afterward."

A little glow was spreading through him. He felt sure she was warming up to him.

"Who told you?"

"Mayor Crump," he answered.

"He told you he was relieved that Lem was gone?" Could that be a trace of bitterness in her voice?

"He said he'd had some trouble with him," Bud said cautiously.

"What did he say about me?" A flash of impatience showed in her eyes at his hesitation. "You asked him about me. Don't deny it."

He grinned. She had a directness that most men lacked. "You're the most attractive woman I've seen in a long time."

She made a slash with the edge of her palm, dismissing what he said. The gesture showed she hadn't been seeking a compliment.

"He told me your name," he said softly.

Her face didn't change. She kept a tough defense about her all the time. "You could have learned that by asking any of my customers," she said tartly. "That's not what I'm asking."

"Crump said a tough class of customers frequent your saloon."

"Why not?" she snapped. "I serve unwatered drinks and ask no questions. My prices are fair. What am I supposed to do? Screen every customer before I let him in?"

Bud held up his hands. "Lord, Lilah, I'm not making any demands on you. How you run your business is none of my concern, as long as you don't break the laws."

She sniffed. "That stupid old man doesn't think that way. If he had his way, I think he'd like to see me run out of town."

"I don't know what's in his head," Bud said slowly, "but I know one thing. He won't get any help from me."

She gave him a flash of those magnificent eyes. "You know, I think you mean that."

"I do," he said huskily.

She posed a direct question. "What if Crump gave you a direct order to close me up and run me out of town?"

"It wouldn't do him any good," Bud said decisively. "Unless he had solid reasons. I don't have to obey orders that come from twisted thinking."

She stared at him for a long moment. "I think we'll get along," she said softly.

Bud laughed deep in his throat. "Thanks."

"What are you going to do about the Mallory family?"

His forehead wrinkled in puzzlement. "I don't know what you mean."

"Lem has two brothers. I know them. They'll come after you. They're not as good with a gun as Lem was, but there's two of them."

"I did hear about them," he confessed. "But they haven't come after me yet. Maybe they've decided not to try."

Lilah shook her head. "They can't let their brother's killing drop. They live on a small farm some twenty miles out of town. It'll take a little time for them to get here. You just keep your eyes open."

Bud couldn't tell her that he wouldn't know them if they popped up right before him. But she was concerned for him, and the thought warmed him. "I won't get careless," he promised. "Maybe I can talk some sense into them."

"Don't depend on that," she warned. "They're like Lem, hardheaded and obstinate."

Bud started to answer, but a big, bluff voice interruped him. "Hello, Lilah. Did you think I'd never get back?"

Bud whirled to face the speaker. He saw a large, rough looking man with a full beard, and for an instant Bud didn't recognize him. But something vaguely familiar about him gnawed at Bud. He couldn't explain the quick springing anger that enveloped him. Maybe the interruption was enough to arouse his anger.

"Mister," he said steadily, "you're interrupting a private conversation."

"Now ain't that real tough?" the man jeered. He threw back and laughed uproariously. The way he laughed and the sight of all that gold in his mouth hit Bud like a swung fist. Hell yes, he knew this man, but it had been years ago. He hadn't liked this person any better than than he did now.

That scene of eight years ago crawled back into Bud's mind. It was odd how moments of terror lasted, particularly when they were bolstered with an ever increasing memory. Bud had had the hell beaten out of him by Toby Watkins, a big lumbering kid five or six years older than him. It had happened in a schoolyard where Bud was eating lunch. He had saved a piece of cake for last, and Toby had sauntered by and snatched it from his hand.

"You give that back," Bud had howled in indignation.

"Make me," Toby taunted.

Bud had tried, but he was a poor match from the start. At that age, he was a scrawny kid and underdeveloped. No wonder Toby didn't recognize him now. Bud had tried to take back the piece of cake, and Toby had easily held him back with an outthrust right hand. He held the cake in his left hand, and while Bud had struggled to get past that restraint, Toby had taken a huge bite out of the piece of cake.

Bud's rage had wiped out all reasoning power. It didn't matter that Toby was older and bigger. The only thought in Bud's mind was to hurt him. Toby was a big dolt of a kid, and should have been out of school several years ago, but that dull mind didn't seem to be able to assimilate anything. He had been put back year after year, and at the rate he was going he would be a man in middle life before he graduated.

Toby's attention was momentarily diverted while he finished the cake. Bud took advantage of the moment to slip by the huge, restraining hand. He got close enough to Toby to swing a wild right hand. His aim wasn't the best, but the fist did glance off Toby's cheek. It must have stung because Toby threw back his head and howled. Bud couldn't think of anything that gave him greater pleasure.

Toby pulled his head down between his shoulders and advanced menacingly toward Bud. "That's gonna cost you," he threatened.

Bud had hit him once and hurt him, and maybe that gave him too much false courage: he could do it again, and he tried. But Toby now had both hands to fend him off, and this time Bud couldn't get close. He kept trying to advance, but each approach ran into a big fist that knocked him back and made his head spin.

The fight drew the rest of the kids, and they formed a noisy, shouting circle about the contestants. Bud's head rang so badly he couldn't make out who they were shouting encouragement to. One of his eyes was closing, and his vision was getting more and more hazy. He leaked blood from his nose, and one lip was split. The only thing that wasn't getting weaker about him was his rage. Each time Toby hurt him, it added fuel to his anger. He didn't care how long it took, or how much punishment he took, he was going to get even with Toby.

Bud went down three times, and each time he was sure there wasn't enough strength in his arms to lift his battered body from the ground. Toby's taunting spurred Bud to make another effort to rise.

The noise must have attracted the teacher, for she came out and broke up the fight.

"This is disgraceful," she stormed. "Stop this immediately."

Bud struggled to get at Toby until he recognized the voice of authority. It added to his sense of disgrace to have the teacher come out and see how beaten he was. Now all his rage was gone, and he hung his head. He only wanted to cry, and he couldn't allow that.

"Who started this?" the teacher demanded.

"He did," Toby answered.

"You're a liar," Bud said furiously. He surged forward, and it took all the teacher's strength to hold him back."

"Stop it, Bud," she cried. "Stop it this minute."

Bud had never heard her sound so tough, and he hung his head again. "Yes, ma'am," he said meekly. "He stole my cake."

"Toby, did you steal his cake?" she asked.

A half-dozen voices answered the question. "He did, Miss Marshall. We saw him."

Her voice grew more severe. "You've been nothing but a source of trouble, Toby. I'm going to talk to your father

and see if he won't take you out of school. You're not doing any good here."

Her words emboldened Toby. "Do you think I care?"
he shouted.

"That's enough, Toby," she said firmly. "You can go
home now." She turned to Bud, and she looked concerned.
"Your face is so bloody, Bud." Her voice was distressed.
"Come with me, and I'll help you clean up."

"You don't have to," he muttered.

"But I want to. No more arguments, Bud."

It took a good twenty minutes before she was satisfied
with her work. "That's a little better, Bud." Her voice
trembled. "The bleeding's almost stopped. Why did you
fight with him? You knew he's so much bigger. Didn't you
thing this could happen?"

"I had to, Miss Marshall," he said earnestly. "He
snatched the piece of cake I was saving. Can't you see I
had to?"

"I can see," she said softly. "Bud, would you like to go
home now? Or you can lie down until you feel better."

He wanted to tell her he didn't feel bad, but that would
be an outright lie. "I guess I want to go home," he said
weakly.

"Don't come back until you feel like it." She pressed
his shoulders, and that gesture of sympathy made him feel
like bawling again.

Emory looked at Bud's battered face in amazement.
"What the hell happened to you?"

Bud wished he could avoid telling Emory, but the only
way to do that was to lie. He had never been a good liar,
particularly where his father was concerned.

"I got in a fight with Toby," he said. "He stole my piece
of cake."

Emory didn't question his reason for fighting. "That big,
awkward kid?"

Bud nodded.

"He sure beat the hell out of you," Emory observed.
"But with his size, that's nothing to be ashamed about."

Bud looked at his reflection in a mirror. This was the

first time he had seen the results of the fight. "Pa, I look like a scarecrow," he wailed.

Emory draped an arm over his shoulders. "Pretty close to it," he said and chuckled.

"Pa, do I have to go back to school tomorrow?"

Emory's face turned stern. "Do you have a good reason for not going?"

"The way I look, Pa. If Toby starts riding me again, I don't think I could stand it."

Emory understood immediately what Bud meant. "I see," he said reflectively. "How long do you want to stay away?"

"Until my face heals."

Emory pulled at an ear lobe. "That would take at least a week, maybe longer." He pulled Bud to him and hugged him. "The way you look, I don't blame you. Maybe you're a faster healer than we know."

Bud was off a week and a half before the discoloration faded and the cuts healed. His throat was tight as he approached the schoolyard. If that damned Toby jumped him again—He looked down, and his fists were clenched. That said exactly how he felt.

A dozen kids surrounded him, and Bud steeled himself for the first hoot of laughter. It didn't come. One of the kids said, "Bud, did you hear what happened? Toby quit school. I guess Miss Marshall finally persuaded Toby's old man to let him drop out."

The sun was suddenly brighter, the sky bluer. "I'm glad," Bud said fervently. He was getting old enough to realize that most of the things a person worried about never happened.

At the end of the day he found a chance to speak to the teacher. "I'm sorry I missed so much time, Miss Marshall. I'll make it up."

Her eyes twinkled. "I know you will, Bud." She hesitated, then decided to say what was on her mind. "Did all this teach you something, Bud?"

She knew why he hadn't been to school. He didn't want to risk running into Toby again.

"It sure did," he said steadily. "Not to cross bridges before I come to them."

Her pleasure showed in her laughter. "That's it exactly, Bud. Despite all the pain the lesson cost you, I think you'll find it was worth it."

Chapter 6

All the old scenes faded from Bud's mind. After so many years, it seemed he was destined to run across Toby Watkins again. Toby had a quarrelsome nature. He wouldn't leave because Bud told him to. They would be fighting over Lilah. In a way, it would be a duplication of the first fight. Bud felt a knot of worry in his belly. It could happen again. But there was an eagerness chewing away at the hard core of worry. It didn't have to happen that way. He was older and had filled out. He had the experience of several other confrontations. In a few words, he had grown up.

Toby was older than Bud, but that no longer mattered. Bud evaluated the change in Toby. That additional weight wasn't important. A lot of it was fat. Maybe Bud got confidence from the authority of his badge. He didn't know about that. He was only sure he wasn't backing down.

"I said this was a private conversation—" Bud cut off saying the name. He had almost called this man by name.

Toby glared at Bud. "Are you looking for trouble, Marshal?" He slurred the title, making an insult of it.

"Any way you want it," Bud said.

Toby blinked in surprise. The man he faced wasn't awed by his size. "Hell, I'm not fighting you," he blustered. "You'd use that badge and arrest me. Besides, you're carrying a gun. I'm not armed." He lifted his arms from his sides.

. Bud unbuckled his gun belt, then laid it on the bar. He half smiled at Lilah. "I'd appreciate you keeping an eye on this."

For a moment, there had been a rapport between them, for her eyes were soft and almost melting. Now they looked blankly at him as though she had never seen him before.

Disappointment led his anger as he looked back at Toby. "Anytime you're ready."

Toby roared and leaped at Bud. He was big, with the power that went with his size, but he was on the clumsy side and didn't handle his weight very well. He swung a ponderous fist at Bud, and it whistled through the air. It might have ripped Bud's head off if it had landed, but Bud ducked and the fist went harmlessly over his head. Toby's momentum carried him on past.

Bud straightened, and he was behind Toby. The target was too inviting for him to pass up. He cocked his fist and landed it on the back of Toby's exposed neck. Toby's startled grunt was half pain, half roar. The force of the blow sent him straight toward the bar. With each foot he covered, he bent lower and lower. He crashed into the bar, and his weight was a formidable force.

Bud heard the splintering of wood. He glanced at Lilah, smiling apologetically.

Toby's head didn't go clear through the bar. He put his hands against the wood, pushed at it, and his head came free. The combined force of the blow and the impact had dazed him. Most of his strength seemed drained. He half turned toward Bud, his eyes vague and wondering. He tried to take a step, and his legs refused to support him. He sat down hard, his expression bewildered.

"You pushed this," Bud said calmly. "Now get up."

Toby made no effort to move. He just stared at Bud puzzledly.

Bud's voice hardened. "I said get up." At Toby's lack of compliance, he stepped forward and drove the pointed toe of his boot into Toby's thigh. The kick pulled a half sob, half scream from Toby. Bud got pleasure from the sound. It brought back the schoolyard fight. Emory had always told him that getting in the first blow was seventy-five per- cent of a fight. If what Emory said was true, Bud had the advantage.

The murderous glare came back into Toby's eyes. "Why, damn you," he howled. "I'm going to make you damned sorry for that."

Bud grinned. "You can try."

Toby had to make a second attempt to get back on his feet. Maybe Bud was giving away some advantage by let- ting him get up, but he wanted to prove to Toby and him- self that he was man enough to handle Toby in a fight.

Toby made it to his feet and leaned against the bar, panting hard. The impact with the solid wood had split the skin on his forehead, and blood trickled slowly down his face.

Bud risked another glance at Lilah. She had the most impassive face he had ever seen. If she had any thoughts about this fight, she kept them masked.

Toby blew his nose, hunched up his shoulders, then slowly shuffled forward. He kept his face hidden behind his forearms; evidently he didn't like punishment in the face. This wasn't a smart fighter. He protected one area and left another unguarded. Bud had to teach him that a man could be hurt wherever he was hit.

Bud darted in, getting off a blow before Toby even thought of letting one go. He sank his fist deep into Toby's belly, and an explosive release of breath fanned his cheek. The blow hurt Toby. His face contorted, and he lowered his arms to cover the abused area. His eyes were glazed, and a slight tinge of green showed in his face.

Bud couldn't pass this advantage. He glided in and drove a fist into Toby's nose. It wasn't a fight-ending blow, but it hurt. Add up several punishing blows like this, and it sapped the heart out of a man.

Toby bled like a stuck hog. Blood gushed from his mashed nose, stained the lower half of his face, and flowed onto his shirt. He looked ghastly with that bloody mask.

Bud glanced at Lilah. Maybe all this bloody release would dismay her. She watched, her eyes alert, but he couldn't read any emotion on her face.

The broken nose and the bleeding made a travesty of Toby's voice. "Damn you," he repeated in a voice several notes higher. "You'll be damned sorry before this is over."

"I'm not sorry yet," Bud said mockingly.

Toby wiped the back of a hand across his nose, smearing his face further. He drew a deep breath and spit out a gout of blood.

Bud watched him carefully. Toby wasn't badly hurt yet, and he was beginning to think. He should be beginning to wonder if what he got out of this fight was worth all the trouble and hurt.

Bud wanted to jar him. "Don't you know, me, Toby?" he jeered. "Don't you remember the day you beat the hell out of me in the schoolyard? You stole a piece of cake from me. When I tried to get it back, you really came down on me."

Recognition flooded Toby's eyes. "Bud Carson," he wheezed. "I did it before. Now I'll do it again."

That mocking note returned to Bud's voice. "You haven't done anything yet, have you?" Maybe recalling that old memory could be a stimulus to Toby, but Bud wanted to take that chance. He wanted Toby to know who was knocking him around.

Toby wiped his nose once again, then, gathering all his strength, come with a rush. Bud's eyes narrowed at the renewed vitality. Maybe he had made a mistake. He kept slipping away from those maddened charges, blocking a punch here, ducking under another there. So far, he hadn't attempted to hit Toby again. He was content to let Toby expend all his energy in these futile charges.

His retreat carried him about the room, and things were still going well. In fact, he was enjoying this. Toby was beginning to show the effects of this useless expenditure of energy. His rushes weren't nearly as determined, and he was wheezing hard. The labored gasps carried plainly to Bud.

Maybe he had played his cat-and-mouse game long

enough. Bud abruptly stopped his retreat and lashed out with his left hand. He bounced the fist off of Toby's fore-head, and it rocked the man's head back. Bud stung him again with four, quick blows. Each of them found its tar-get, and each demanded its toll. But none of them was a finishing blow. Bud wanted to save that a little longer. Alarm was beginning to fill Toby's eyes, and his footsteps were slow. He dragged his feet across the floor, and each foot was suddenly very heavy.

Bud heard the rumble of voices in the room. From the tone of them he couldn't tell whether or not they were pleased with his winning. He wished he could get a look at Lilah. He would like to know how she was taking this. Toby kept shaking his head as though he was trying to es-cape from the gnawing pain. With each shake, drops of blood flew. Bud's fists had cut him to pieces.

Bud was suddenly sickened of this bloody game. He had collected more than enough to pay him for an ancient fight. It was time to finish it.

"All right, Toby," he said. "It's done." He stepped for-ward.

Somebody kicked his leading foot out from under him. In his absorption with Toby, Bud didn't see who did it. All he knew was that a supporting leg was whipped out from under him. He fell heavily, striking a cheekbone against the floor. The impact was hard enough to scatter his senses. His eyes watered, and his thoughts reeled.

The sound of heavy feet jerked him from that dizzying spell. His eyes still didn't focus well, but he could see the bulk of a figure rushing at him. Even though he couldn't see him plainly, it had to be Toby. He rolled quickly and was just in time for the sole of a boot scraped his shoul-der. If it had been on the target Toby wanted, it probably would have kicked his head off. There was enough force in that scraping contact to make him grind his teeth to-gether. He set his mind against the enveloping pain and kept rolling. Each time that shoulder touched the floor, Bud felt a stab of pain.

Toby stomped after him, swearing deep in his throat, trying to kick him again. But each time he stopped and planted himself, Bud rolled enough so that the kick had no time for contact.

Toby was never very bright. If Bud had been in his place, and Toby was rolling about on the floor, he wouldn't have tried to kick him. He would have dived on him, smothering him against the floor with his weight. He grimaced at the thought. It was a good thing for him that Toby was such a slow thinker.

Bud rolled under a pool table, and that gave him the space he needed to get back to his feet. He stood and glared fiercely at the crowd. "Anybody tries to kick my feet from under me again, I'll knock his damned head off."

All eyes shifted away from him, and he couldn't be sure who the culprit was. But he thought that stunt wouldn't be tried again.

Meanwhile, Toby was lumbering around the pool table, panting audibly in his eagerness to get at Bud again.

"You lost your chance, Toby," Bud said and planted himself squarely. He ducked Toby's awkward blows and stepped in to get all the leverage he could into the blow. He tried to bury his fist in Toby's belly, and this blow was more savage than the first one. The breath whooshed out of Toby, and that green color seeped into his face again. He doubled over without a thought of trying to protect his jaw, and Bud aimed at the exposed target. This time he wanted the fight ended, and he got the weight of his shoulder behind the blow. He landed it squarely against the whiskered jaw, feeling the shock of the impact run from his knuckles clear up into his shoulder. He winced at the stabbing pain as a knuckle buckled. Bud didn't know how bad the hurt was, but he doubted he would be able to use that hand again tonight.

The blow straightened Toby up, and his eyes rolled back into his head. He swayed like a tree that had been deeply undercut, then slowly toppled. He gained momentum as he fell, and he crashed on his face. His arms were outflung before him, and Bud watched them closely to see if there was a flicker of life in them. They didn't move. He drew several hard breaths to ease his laboring lungs, then moved slowly to the motionless figure. He put a boot toe under Toby's torso, moved the foot, and the body turned over.

Bud looked at the exposed face. Lord, what a mess he had made of those features. That was more than atonement for the beating Bud had taken. Toby was unconscious. His mouth was open with his labored breathing, but the eyelids didn't raise.

Bud walked up to the bar and strapped on his gun belt. "Seems like I'm always messing up your floor," he tried to say humorously. He anxiously watched those opaque eyes. He wished there was some way for him to know what was going on behind them.

"Yes," Lilah agreed. "I'd be just as happy if you didn't come back in here again."

Bud couldn't tell which emotion was behind the words, anger or resignation. Lilah stared at him, and her eyes were beginning to fire up. He sighed, and his shoulders slumped. He wasn't making much progress with her at all. Her face was implacable as she waited for him to say something.

"Well, good night," Bud said weakly. He looked back from the door. Lilah stared after him, and her smooth face was rock hard. He couldn't see Toby. The crowd had gathered around him. They could add the fight to Lem's shooting. The two things would give them enough to talk about for weeks to come.

Chapter 7

Toby's eyelids flutttered, and he groaned several times before he opened his eyes. He looked about him wildly, not recognizing his surroundings. His eyes swept around the room and rested on the woman sitting behind the desk.

"Lilah," he said huskily. "Where am I?" He raised a hand and brushed it across his face. The hand came away wet. "It feels like I was caught out in a rain," he grumbled.

She watched him almost indifferently, neither concern nor compassion in her face. "I threw water in your face. You're in my office. The only rain you were in was a rain of fists."

Comprehension lit up his eyes. Things were coming back to him now. He touched his face and groaned again. He hurt every place his fingers touched.

"That marshal was pretty good," he said weakly. "I never been up against anybody who used his fists as good or moved so well."

Lilah still watched him with judgment in her eyes. "You asked for it. You could have backed away, but you kept pushing."

"He made me sore." Toby ran his tongue around the inside of his mouth and winced. Damned if he didn't have cuts there, too. "Hanging over you the way he did, I wanted to teach him a lesson."

Lilah's mouth hardened. Every time Toby got this possessive note in his tone, her lips were a thin, cruel line. Why in the hell had she been so foolish as to marry him? Too young, she guessed. He was far more attractive then, and they had worked well as a team. "You knew him?" she snapped.

Toby sat up and groaned at the hurt the effort caused him. "I did. For a brief while. That was back in school. We got in a fight. I knocked the hell out of him then."

Lilah smiled mercilessly. "You sure didn't this time."

Toby winced, and this time it was at the spiritual hurt, not the physical. "He had the advantage tonight. He's a marshal, and I didn't know how he'd use this fight against me. I didn't want him arresting me." He saw no relenting in Lilah's harsh, judging look, and sought for another excuse that might make her let up on him. "He had a gun, and I didn't know for sure if he'd try to use it."

Lilah's lips curled in disgust. She hadn't known until after they were married that Toby was such a weak man. With each new month of married life, that weakness became more apparent. She had left him several times, but the physical attraction had always been too much. Each time she had allowed him back.

"He took the gun off and left it on the bar," she pointed out. "You knew he wasn't going to use it. No, at first you thought you could take him."

Toby stared angrily at her. "I didn't," he said defensively. "Hell, you had a gun behind the bar. When you saw I was losing, you could have used it."

Hot color rose in her face. "Do you expect me to fight your battles for you?"

That stung Toby. "You could have stopped him. You could have ordered him out of the saloon."

"You wanted him to arrest me?" Lilah snapped.

Toby pulled at his fingers. The popping of the knuckles was loud in the small office. "Well, no," he said weakly. "You could have told him you didn't allow fighting in your place."

"After he killed Lem Mallory in here?" she jeered. "I

don't want that marshal to turn against me for any reason."

Toby touched his fingers to his face again, and they came away stained. "Hey, I'm still bleeding. Have you got a handkerchief?"

She rummaged in her desk and came up with a piece of cloth. She tossed it to him, and he caught it. He turned it over and said unhappily, "This is nothing but a rag."

"It'll do," she said icily. "Do you think I want my handkerchief stained?"

Toby gingerly dabbed at his cheek. "The next time I go up against him, I'll take him."

"Get that idea out of your head," she said derisively. "You'll only be asking for more of what you got tonight."

"Then I'll get him some other way," Toby snarled. "I'll get him with a gun."

"Don't be such a damned fool as to think you can outshoot him," Lilah jeered. Her laughter was cruel and cutting.

"What's so damned funny?"

"Thinking of you going up against him with a gun. Lem Mallory thought he could win, too. He kept pushing the quarrel until the marshal faced him. He outdrew him. Hit him just under the heart."

Toby's eyes widened. "Lem was tops with a gun. Are you sure the marshal didn't use some kind of a trick that threw Lem off?"

"I saw it all," she said sharply. "He let Lem start for his gun, then beat him fair and square. Lem wanted to run the new law out of town." That merciless smile was on her lips again. "I wonder if Lem knows now how far wrong he was."

A new triumph was in Toby's voice. "I won't have to do anything about the marshal. Lem left two brothers. They'll square his death."

Lilah shook her head in negation. "Those two dolts? Neither of them could hold a candle to Lem. And he couldn't stop the marshal."

"But there's two of them," Toby objected.

"It won't make any difference," Lilac said with finality.

"Unless they ambush him, and I doubt if they can even make that work."

Toby was curious. "You sound as though you hope he stays around." His expression turned mean. "Say! Is there something going on between you two?"

The rawness of her expression appalled him. "I've had all the experience I want with men by being married to you. You dumb fool. Can't you see that he might be protection for me?"

Toby still looked sullen. She had made her feelings about him plain. It had been over two months since he had touched her. But maybe she had a point here. With a deputy marshal honeying around her, nobody could think of questioning what she was doing.

"That could be smart," he said grudgingly.

"How would you know?" she sneered.

Toby flushed and said plaintively, "Aw, Lilah. You're always on me. Nothing I do suits you."

She waved away his complaining. "Did you get rid of those horses?"

"I did, Lilah." By holding onto the desk, he clambered to his feet. He pulled a wad of money out of his pocket.

Her eyes glistened at the size of the roll. The sight of money always touched Lilah. "It looks as though you did all right," she said reluctantly.

Toby beamed his pleasure. "I think I did, Lilah. But the men ain't been paid yet."

Five men including himself worked for Lilah. Six weeks ago they had made a raid on old man Kaiser's big south pasture, running off twenty of his fine brood mares. Lem had played it smart in getting them out of Oklahoma. He only allowed the horses to be driven a few hours in the middle of the night.

"No trouble?" she asked. Her attention wasn't fully on him. She was counting the money, her eyes gleaming.

Toby shook his head. "No trouble. I didn't take them to Colorado."

Her face stiffened as she carefully laid down the money. "What?" she exploded.

Toby's face was uneasy. "No. I heard the market had

gone to hell in Colorado. I decided to run them down to the Texas Panhandle. They were looking for horses down there. That's why I got such a good price." He preened himself like a rooster before an admiring hen. He expected praise, and his face showed it.

Instead, Lilah was furious. Toby's face fell. He never knew which way Lilah was going to jump.

"You think I did wrong?" he asked uneasily.

"You could have," she said, thin lipped. "That's Texas Ranger country. A bunch of horses that big is bound to arouse some attention. You know what would have happened if the Rangers had caught you?"

He knew. His neck was suddenly tight as though a brutal constriction was around it. "Well, they didn't find me," he said sullenly. "Nobody asked any questions."

She counted out some of the bills and shoved them toward him. "That's for the men and you. You know the old Grimes' place?"

"That old run-down house?" Toby asked. "Nobody's been near it for years."

"That's why nobody will look for you there. I want you to stay out there until I'm sure how this comes out. Old Kaiser is still raising hell about his missing horses."

Toby folded the money and thrust it in his pocket, careful not to let her see the resentful gleam in his eyes. He hadn't missed the size of the pile of money she'd laid out for herself. It hadn't been that way when they started; it had been fifty-fifty then. Now she took the lion's share, and her eyes seemed to dare him to comment unfavorably on the division.

Before he knew it things had been completely out of control, and he had wound up the underdog. It was an unnatural situation between a man and a woman. He wouldn't admit he was afraid of her, not even to himself, but he'd change that. One of these days he was going to slap some sense into her head and take his rightful position.

Toby was careful not to stare directly at Lilah, for fear she would see the resentment bubbling up in his eyes. He had allowed her to get too powerful, and there was nothing much he could do about it now. But that would change when the opportune moment came.

"Lilah, is there anything you want me to do now?"

"Just stay at the Grimes' place until I get in touch with you."

There were those damned orders again. "How long will that be?"

"How do I know?" she flared. "When I see something that can turn us a few pennies, I'll get word to you." Toby started for the door, and she stopped him. "Another thing, Toby. Don't you and the boys hand around the saloon any more."

His suspicions rekindled. She was trying to hide something. There must be something going on between her and that damned marshal. If he had any proof of that, he would take care of both of them. "Lilah, kicking the boys and me out will cost you a lot of money. We did all our drinking in here before. Now——" He spread his hands and shrugged. "Some other place will get all that patronage."

She stared impassively back at him. "Not if you stay at the Grimes' place. Toby, you build yourself up too much. You didn't spend that much money." She dismissed him with a wave of her hand. "Go on, get out of here. I'll get in touch with you when I need you."

Lilah watched the door close behind Toby, and her rage increased. Toby was overrating his importance to her. She was going to have to get rid of him one of these days. Maybe sooner than he anticipated. But with that new marshal around, she would have to be careful of every move. She smiled faintly. She wasn't really worried about the marshal. She saw the way he looked at her. She could handle him.

Chapter 8

Bud and Billy were just finishing cleaning up the office. The floor had been scrubbed, and the walls washed down. It looked livable.

"What do you think?" Billy asked anxiously.

Bud draped an arm across the boy's shoulders. "It looks good to me."

Billy sighed in relief. He had worked hard. "Will Crump think so?"

"He will," Bud said positively. "He has to. He gave me the money I put out on this office."

Billy whistled in amazement. "What did you use on that old skinflint to make him cough up?"

Bud shook his head. "You don't show much respect for our mayor."

"I will when he earns it," Billy said flatly. "You going to paint the walls?"

"Nor for a while. They don't look so bad."

At Billy's crestfallen appearance Bud asked, "Are you that eager to start?"

"It's not that," Billy muttered. "When the work stops, so does my job."

"Not yet," Bud disagreed. "I plan to keep you around for some time. Besides, you haven't pointed out the Mallory brothers to me."

Billy's face brightened. "I haven't, have I? I been look-

61

ing all over town for them. Nobody's seen them. But they'll show up. The Mallorys carry a grudge real well. They'll be burning to avenge Lem." He cut his eyes at Bud. "But that don't worry you. You like trouble."

Bud pursed his lips. "What gives you that fool idea?"

Billy grinned. "If you don't go looking for it, it sure finds you. I heard you got in another fight last night, with that Toby Watkins. That right?"

Bud grimaced. This kid had big ears, and he picked up a lot of information. "You heard right. But I didn't push the fight, Toby did. I finally had to oblige him. He wasn't armed. I took my gun off and used my fists."

Billy speculatively eyes him. "You sound like it gave you a lot of satisfaction."

"It did," Bud said reflectively. "He kicked the hell out of me once. That happened quite a few years ago while both of us were in school. Toby was always a big, swaggering kid, older and bigger than I was. He kind of had it in for me, and he kept pushing at me until I had to fight him."

He grinned at Billy. "Stay out of all the fights you can. You can avoid a lot of lumps that way."

"But you whipped him," Billy insisted.

Bud shook his head. "No, I didn't. Not the first time. The school marm came out and stopped it. I think Toby would have beat me to pieces if she hadn't. She sent Toby home."

"Did you ever fight him again?"

"Not until last night. I never saw him again until then. Toby dropped out of school. I didn't go back for several days. I didn't want the other kids seeing me."

"Why? He hurt you that bad?"

Bud sighed. Billy had a big nose, and he wasn't going to stop poking it in until he was satisfied he had all the details.

"I wasn't hurt that bad," Bud said patiently. "He marked me up pretty good, and I didn't want the kids seeing me like that. I never saw him again until last night. I had a lot to collect from him. I left him cold on the floor."

"I bet you enjoyed that," Billy commented.

Bud reflectively rubbed his swollen knuckle. It was tender. He wouldn't be able to put too much pressure on it for several days. "I sure did, Billy," Bud said, and grinned. "If Toby wants to pick up that fight, I'd be glad to oblige him."

Billy looked at him with awe. "I'm glad you're not mad at me."

Bud chuckled. "You wouldn't do anything to make me mad at you." He started to add something, and a man coming in the door interrupted him.

He was a dumpy little figure, and encroaching age had nibbled away at the fluidity of his walk. He was round-faced and clean-shaven except for a goatee.

"You the new marshal?" the man demanded, even though he could see the badge on Bud's vest.

Bud kept his temper. He answered calmly enough, "I'm the marshal. What can I do for you?"

"I doubt if you can do anything," the man said spitefully. "I never saw a lawman that's worth what he's paid."

Bud could feel that heat rising in his cheeks. This was the kind that was the hardest to handle. They made preconceived judgments and stubbornly refused to think them over. Age made them hold on harder than ever to those judgments.

"Whoa, back up," Bud managed to say calmly. "Suppose we start off by telling our names. I'm Bud Carson, sent down here to give a hand." His eyes stabbed at the old man, daring him to ignore what he just said.

The old man blinked and spluttered. His mouth slowly opened as he evaluated the marshal. "I'm Ed Kaiser."

Bud thrust out his hand. "I'm glad to know you, Ed. What can I do for you?"

Kaiser took Bud's hand, but there was no warmth in his grip. "Nothing, I suppose," he said grumpily. "None of your kind has done any good yet."

Bud winked at Billy, who was watching the clash open mouthed. "Suppose you simmer down, Mr. Kaiser, and tell me what this is all about."

Kaiser was a hardheaded man. "I told the last sheriff about it. I raised hell. It didn't do any good."

"I'm not that sheriff," Bud said sharply. "How can I do any good if I don't even know what you're talking about?"

The words were direct and harsh. Kaiser blinked and spluttered. Bud recognized the signs. The old man was ready to lose his temper when Bud said, "Go on. Blow your top. All you'll accomplish is to waste your time and mine." He grinned at the struggle Kaiser made to control himself. This was a tough old rooster, and apparently he hadn't often been crossed.

Bud shoved the one chair toward him. "Sit down, Mr. Kaiser. I'm ready to listen to your problem when you're ready to quit spitting and talk sanely."

Kaiser's face crimsoned, and Bud held up an arresting hand. "I told you that won't do you any good."

Bud sat on the corner of the desk, watching Kaiser trying to talk coherently. Kaiser would glare at him, look away quickly, then make another attempt. "You'd be mad, too, if what happened to me happened to you," he growled.

"I don't doubt it," Bud said gravely. "The trouble is that I don't know what happened to you." His eyes twinkled. "I don't even know how mad to get."

"Young whippersnapper!" Kaiser spewed. "I had some horses stole," he finally managed to get out. "They came right into my pasture and stole them almost from under my nose."

Bud nodded. "That's more than enough to make any man mad," he said soberly. "I couldn't have controlled my temper half as well as you have. I'd have been raving and cussing all over town."

The harsh, thin line of Kaiser's mouth was slowly melting, and his eyes were softening. Bud was slowly winning the old man over.

"Yes, siree," Kaiser went on. "Twenty mares. As good breeding stock as you would ever want to see. The buyer was to pick them up next week, then those thieving bastards hit me."

"Where did this happen, Mr. Kaiser?"

"At my place. I breed horses about twenty miles out of town. Billy, you know where my place is."

Billy nodded eagerly. "I sure do, Mr. Kaiser. Never saw a purtier place."

That pleased the old man, and he gave the kid a frosty grin. "Try to keep it that way. Spent all of my life building it up." Color suffused his face again. "Then those thieving bastards snuck in—"

But held up a hand to check the growing tirade. He was never going to get the details if he couldn't keep Kaiser calmed down.

"When did it happen, Mr. Kaiser?"

"At night. That big pasture is a couple of miles from the house. Too far away for me to hear a damned thing."

"Do you keep any help out there, Mr. Kaiser?"

"Of course I do. Think an old man can run a horse farm by his self? I keep three hands. All good men."

Bud kept a hard clamp on his patience. It was going to be hard to get this story out of Kaiser as worked up as he was. He would have to dig to get a fact here, a fact there. But then, he couldn't blame the old man too much. Kaiser had suffered a considerable loss.

"Did you discover the loss the day after it happened?"

Kaiser scowled ferociously at him as somehow he found Bud to blame. "I don't exactly know what night they were took. In the summer I might go several days before I check that pasture."

Bud sighed. "Go on, Mr. Kaiser."

"I figure it happened on a Tuesday night," Kaiser continued. "Me and Clyde went out there the following Sunday. The pasture was empty. We found tracks—lots of tracks."

Bud relaxed. Now maybe he was getting somewhere. "Could you figure out how many drove the horses away?"

Kaiser frowned. "It was either four or five."

"Could you track them?"

Kaiser shook his head, an unhappy look on his face. "We tried. We tracked them for a couple of days. Lost them in a wide band of rocky land. Every now and then we picked up another track and that encouraged us to go on, but it'd take another hour or two to pick up the next one. I figured we was losing too much time in reporting the theft."

Bud nodded. "That was wise. Which direction did they go?"

Kaiser scowled in perplexity. "They started west, then gradually swung to the south. South was the last direction we could figure out."

It was Bud's time to frown. "If you knew of the loss on Sunday, it had to be almost a week ago. Today's Saturday. Why didn't you come in and report it before?"

Kaiser howled in outrage. "A week ago, hell! When I found the horses gone, it was a little better than six weeks ago."

Bud stared helplessly at him. "Christ, you waited all this time? What held you up so long? With that much lead, I doubt if anybody can find a trace of them. Of all the fool—"

"Hold it," Kaiser yelped. "I reported it to the sheriff who was in this office then. I never did think he was worth much. Shortly after I reported it, he turned in his badge. I only came in to report it now because you're a new man, and you might be able to do some good. From your excuses, I can see I was wrong."

Bud stared at him in utter disbelief. Kaiser was reporting a theft that was already six weeks old. The hope of finding any trail had long ago faded. Yet Kaiser expected him to do something. He started to utter a flat refusal, then held it. Kaiser already had a low opinion of lawmen. A refusal now would only strengthen it.

"I'll try to get out there this afternoon," he said.

Kaiser snorted. "What for? The horses are gone."

It was hard to talk to this old man without losing your temper. "You might have overlooked something that I can spot," Bud said carefully. "It won't do any harm, will it?"

Kaiser got up from the chair. "It won't do any good, either," he said spitefully. He stalked out of the door, his shoulders squared indignantly.

When the door closed Billy said, "Hard to talk to his kind."

"Always is," Bud agreed. "Want to take a trip with me this afternoon?"

Billy walked to the window and stared out of it. "What good could I do?"

"You could show me the way."

"You never know what old Kaiser will do," Billy said doubtfully. "He's liable to take a scatter-gun and run us off his place."

Bud grinned in spite of himself. "Somehow I doubt that. He's like a bad-tempered dog—does more barking than biting."

Billy kept staring out the window, and Bud thought he didn't hear him. Maybe Billy was seeking an excuse to avoid the trip. "If you don't want to go, Billy, I'll manage."

Billy beckoned him to come to the window, and there was a furtiveness in the gesture. He motioned for Bud to stand to one side of the window.

Bud was filled with curiosity. Whatever Billy had in mind, he wasn't making it very plain.

"Across the street," Billy said in a low voice. "The Mallory brothers are here. Jonse and Deke."

Bud risked a quick glance from the side of the window. Two men stood across the street, their interest focused on the small building. One resembled Lem. He had the same sullen attitude, and his head sat on a bull-like neck.

"The big one's Deke," Billy whispered.

Bud's eyes switched to Jonse. There was no resemblance in the brothers. Jonse was skinny and tall with a bullet shaved head. Each was stamped with the same dull-looking meanness—even at this distance. Bud caught the speculation in their scrutiny of the building.

"Are you gonna go out after them?" Billy asked excitedly.

"Why should I?" Bud asked. "I can't arrest them for anything. Standing out there, looking at this building breaks no laws."

"They ain't out there for no good reason," Billy argued.

"Probably not," Bud agreed. "But I'll let them make the first move."

Billy shook his head in disapproval.

The Mallory brothers stayed out there for a good thirty minutes. Bud saw them say something to each other, then turn and amble down the street.

"You don't think I handled that right?" Bud said, and grinned.

"I sure don't," Billy said fiercely. "You're gonna meet them again."

"Probably," Bud said lightly. "You're young, Billy. If there's trouble ahead, don't rush into it. Pick your time. Don't let your enemy pick his." He chuckled lightly. By Billy's scowl, he didn't believe that. Bud would wait another half hour, then start the trip to Kaiser's place. He wished he knew what thoughts had run through the Mallorys' heads. It might have given him a sense of security. He sure didn't have any now.

But that sense was rare in a lawman's life.

Chapter 9

Billy rode Charley, his old donkey. "Not much, is he?" he said morosely. "But one of these days, I'll get me a good horse."

Even as diminutive as Lucky was, Bud towered over Billy. "Beats walking," he said lightly.

They didn't speak much on the trip to Kaiser's. The old man must have seen them coming, for he was outside the house waiting as Bud and Billy rode up.

"Well, I'll say one thing for you," he said sourly. "You keep your word."

"How's that?" Bud asked, surprised.

"You said you'd be out today, and here you are."

"Did you doubt me?" Bud asked tartly.

Kaiser grinned wickedly. "I didn't know. You didn't give me no guarantee." He seemed to enjoy needling Bud. "Some of the other lawmen we've had would promise you anything, then forget all about it."

"I'm not that kind," Bud said acidly. He could forsee that things weren't going to go well between him and Kaiser. The old man demanded the impossible, then cussed him out for not achieving it immediately.

"I'd like to see that pasture," Bud said quietly.

"You think it's going to tell you anything?"

"More than I'll learn standing here jawing." Bud couldn't keep the heat in his voice from showing.

Kaiser guffawed and slapped his thigh. "One thing I'll say for you, you ain't afraid to speak up."

The stress didn't leave Bud's voice. "You know any reason why I should be?"

Kaiser cackled again, then bellowed, "Clyde, get out here!"

Bud thought about their conversation while he waited for Clyde to join them. One way to pull a sort of respect out of Kaiser was to be as cussed mean as the old man was. It was something to remember.

Clyde came out, a tall, lanky man. He moved as though his joints didn't fit very well. He had an amiable face with a perpetual grin. A cowlick fell over his forehead, and he was constantly swiping at it.

"You call me, Boss? You want me?"

"I called you, didn't I? Take the marshal out to the horse pasture. He wants to look it over."

Bud decided that Kaiser treated everybody the same way—bad. But Clyde didn't seem to mind. Maybe he had worked for Kaiser so long that he was used to that salty tongue.

"Ain't you coming with us, Mr. Kaiser?" Clyde asked.

"You know this is my nap time."

Clyde grinned unabashed. "Plumb forgot it. Think the marshal will find anything out there that will do any good?"

"I doubt it. None of them have before."

Bud felt his cheeks heat up. The two talked about him as though he wasn't here. Had Clyde been around Kaiser for so long that he had picked up Kaiser's manner?

"Wait until I get my horse, Marshal," Clyde said.

Bud nodded, and Clyde ambled away.

"I know one thing you don't raise here," Bud said.

Kaiser cut his eyes at him. "What's that?"

"Manners," Bud stated. He didn't give a damn how much that offended the old man.

That aroused Kaiser's sense of humor. "You got too thin a skin, Deputy." He turned and walked into the house.

Bud's eyes burned as he watched him go. He probably

wasn't going to do any good on this job, and he didn't give a damn. He was starting off with too much of a handicap against him. No one could expect him to unravel a six-week-old horse stealing case.

Clyde came up on a roan mare. Bud wondered if a horse picked up the traits of its rider. It seemed that way often. The roan was wing-footed, and she sort of shuffled along. Clyde moved in the same manner.

"How do you stand that old man?" Bud asked.

Clyde grinned. "You mean, Mr. Kaiser? Aw, he ain't so bad when you get used to him. He pays good, and he's never missed a payday."

"He's not paying me," Bud growled. It would take far more than Clyde's dubious recommendations to ever convince him that Kaiser was likable. Hell, Bud would settle for the old coot just being bearable.

They rode some two miles, and Clyde swung down and opened a gate to the biggest pasture Bud had looked at in a long time. "Must be eighty acres here."

"Over a hundred," Clyde corrected.

"Were all the horses in here?"

"They missed four head," Clyde answered. His face twisted. "As pretty a bunch of horses as you'd ever want to look at."

"Any brands or distinguishing marks?"

"One that you couldn't see." Clyde grinned, enjoying the moment.

Bud's eyes brightened with interest. "What's that?"

"They were all tattooed on the inside of the upper lip. If you didn't know what you were looking for, you'd overlook it."

Bud was startled. "That's unusual, isn't it?"

"Not in thoroughbreds. Mr. Kaiser made a trip to Kentucky several years ago. He came back with this new-fangled idea of identifying a horse. It sounded good to him, and we started using it."

"He didn't say anything about that," Bud growled.

Clyde chuckled. "He wouldn't unless you asked him directly. He'd claim that was his personal business." He shook his head. "He's always been closed-mouth. The loss of the horses prodded him into squawking."

Bud waited for Clyde to close the gate and clamber up. "Did they use this gate in stealing those horses?"

Clyde shook his head. "They cut the wire between three posts on the far side of the pasture. Left plenty of room to drive them through."

"Must have been a big bunch in on this. Kaiser said five or six."

Clyde nodded again. "That's right. We counted that many tracks."

"Where's the break in this fence?"

"It ain't there any more." At Bud's indignant look, Clyde said, "We had four horses left in the pasture. We repaired the fence. Does that make you unhappy?"

"It sure does. The robbery happened over six weeks ago, and it isn't reported to me until now. You repair the fence, covering all traces of how they got in."

"They used wire cutters," Clyde said promptly. "I looked at those cut wires. The ends were snicked off clean. Does that help you any?"

Bud shook his head. It didn't help much. Wire cutters were in pretty common use. They could be found all over Oklahoma.

"Point out the break when we come to it," Bud ordered. "There might be some tracks around it."

"I doubt it," Clyde disagreed. "We've had three pretty good rains the last six weeks. If there were any tracks, they're washed out by now."

"Oh fine," Bud groaned. "If my worst enemy wanted me to fail, he couldn't have set it up any better. Why in the hell did Kaiser come to me?"

"He wanted those horses back," Clyde ventured.

"From where I stand, he hasn't any more chance than a snowball in hell."

"Better hadn't let him hear you say that."

Bud's patience snapped. "What can he do? Cuss me out?"

Clyde gave him a tight-lipped grin. "He might do that, too."

Bud turned his horse. "Let's get on back. There's no sense wasting any more time."

Either Kaiser had cut his nap short or he couldn't get to sleep, for he was out in front of the house when Bud, Clyde and Billy returned.

"Learn anything?" he asked.

"How in the hell could I?" Bud demanded savagely. "The fence has been repaired and rain has washed out any tracks." He was really getting worked up. "How do you expect a law officer to overcome all that?"

"I thought you'd fail," Kaiser said, with evident satisfaction.

"Particularly when you made sure you kept important information hidden."

Kaiser blinked at him. "What's that supposed to mean?"

"You didn't tell me you tattooed your horses to identify them."

"I thought everybody knew that about thoroughbreds," Kaiser said scornfully.

"I didn't," Bud snapped.

"Hah! So now you can blame your failure on me. I thought it'd turn out this way. You're like all the law officers I've known—worthless!"

Bud was shaking with rage. He had taken a lot of lip from this man. "Get me a list of those tattoos," he snapped.

"What good will that do you?" Kaiser jeered.

"You let me be the judge of that," Bud raged. "Get me that list!"

Bud fumed the whole fifteen minutes Kaiser was gone.

"He's sure got you fired up," Billy observed.

"Drop it, Billy," Bud snapped. He could say that he'd take care of the matter, but that would be a form of boasting. What he had in mind would take time, and he wasn't sure his idea would even work.

Kaiser came back with the list. Bud looked at the piece of paper. Maybe this would help a little. The list was in numerical order. Bud tucked the piece of paper in his pocket and mounted.

"Are you going to let me know how things turn out?"

Kaiser thought he read refusal in Bud's face, for he squalled, "Damn it. I'm the owner. I've got a right to know!"

Bud turned a savage face toward Kaiser. "Just like you
kept me informed. Come on, Billy."

He spurred Lucky, and Billy had to ride hard to catch
up with him.

After a half-dozen attempts to talk to Bud on the way
back to town, Billy gave up. At each try, Bud would grunt
at him or shake his head. His handling at Kaiser's hands
ran over and over through Bud's mind. The only way he
could begin to wipe out those rankling thoughts was to
recover some or all of the horses. Bud shook his head angrily. That was practically an impossibility. If he had all
the luck in the world, he might be able to recover a few.

He smashed a fist against his thigh. Billy glanced at him
questioningly, and Bud shook his head. When he got his
thoughts sorted out and arranged in proper order, maybe
he could tell the kid what was bothering him.

Just how in the hell he was going to go about recover-
ing those horses he didn't know. It was useless riding
about the country, looking for a horse here and there. Bud
wouldn't know one of those animals if one came up and
bit him on the shoulder. The only identification he had
was the list of tattoos, but he couldn't go about pulling out
every horse's upper lip. He grinned wryly as he thought of
the hell a horse owner would raise if he caught Bud looking in his horse's mouth.

His face brightened as a starting point occurred to him.
Marshal Nix had a lot of influence, reaching farther than
the boundaries of Oklahoma. If Bud had to start out on
his own as a rustler, he would say Texas could be the best
market to dispose of stolen horses. Maybe Nix had influence that would reach down there. He might be able to
persuade the Texas Rangers to keep an eye open for
horses that could have been stolen. With all the Rangers
looking, it would widen Bud's scope. He would get a letter
off to Nix tonight. Then all he had to do was to wait and
hope that a bolt of luck would strike him. Bud was in a
far better mood when he turned Lucky over to Little.

Billy decided to leave Charley at the stable, too. He

cocked an appraising eye at Bud and said with astonishing perception, "You feel better now? Want to talk about it?"

Bud chuckled. The longer he knew this kid, the more he was amazed at his insight. "How could you tell?"

"By your looks. You don't look like you're ready to bite my head off."

"Kaiser got my goat," Bud confessed. "He knows everything. He waits until all the evidence is worn out before he reports, then comes to me with his loss. He expects me to fail."

Billy nodded wisely. "I told you Kaiser was tough." He cocked his head to one side. "You ready to give up?"

"Hell no," Bud snapped. "It might take a little time, but I'll get some of his horses back. I want to see the look on his face when I return them."

Billy looked dubious. "You think you can do it?"

"There's an outside chance," Bud said soberly.

It was getting dark. Lights were coming on along the street. Figures moving about lost their distinct outlines until they passed before a light. It wasn't Bud's favorite time of the day—too many shadows, and every one of them could contain a menace to a lawman.

His stomach rumbled, further reminding him the day was wearing thin. "You hungry, Billy?"

"I could eat," Billy admitted.

Bud could take him to his boardinghouse, but he didn't know how Mrs. Edison would accept a guest. Besides, it could be past the supper hour.

"You know of a good restaurant, Billy?"

Billy reflected over that question. "There's only three in town. Fair, poor, and bad."

Bud grimaced. That was a graphic description. "We better try the fair, then."

Billy grinned. "I thought you'd feel that way. We've got to go back, then. It's at the other end of the street."

"Lead the way."

Bud followed Billy closely. At the far end of the block, he thought he detected movement, but it was so vague and shadowy he couldn't be certain. A prickling sensation ran across his skin, warning him. The light was too poor for him to be sure, but that prickling set off a clanging bell of alarm in his mind. The indefinite warning was bolstered by a solid face: The Mallorys were in town, and they had every reason to want him dead. In just that quick glimpse, he thought he had seen a man edge out from the far side of a building, then pull back hastily.

"Slow it down, Billy." The edge in his voice was like an anchor, pulling Billy down to a mere shuffle.

Bud watched the edge of the building, waiting for confirmation of another movement. He was beginning to argue with the veracity of his eyes. Had he actually seen movement, or had imagination taken over?

He didn't actually see the flash of the gun, but it was instantly followed by the deep cough of a gun. It came from the opposite side of the street.

Bud knew immediately what had happened. He wasn't hit, and he sprang forward, his hands outstretched. He caught Billy in the back, and the force of his hands shoved Billy off his feet. Billy went down hard, his startled grunt hanging in the air.

Bud dove off his feet. He hit on a shoulder and rolled, a hand grabbing for the butt of his gun. He came to a halt, his eyes flicking from one side of the street to the other. It was a well-laid ambush, and he tried to cover both sides of the street at once.

"Stay down, Billy," he hissed. Damn this poor light. If only he could see what was going on.

Another lance of flame came from the side of the street where he had first detected movement. Either his rolling or the surprise of how this was turning out had affected the ambusher's aim, for the shot was wide. Bud saw the gout of dirt a good three feet from him.

The flame momentarily lit the dark bulk of a figure, standing clear of the building. Bud fired at that brief flash, and heard a grunt that broke into a high, bubbling scream. He didn't wait to see the figure fall. He threw himself to one side, his attention going across the street. The second brother would take over the ambush. He prayed that Billy had enough sense to keep pressed tightly against the dirt.

Another shot rang out. Bud's teeth were clenched so

tightly his jaws ached. The bullet gouged a hole in the ground behind him. The flame was instantly gone, but Bud had its position locked in his mind's eye. He fired once, then again, and a third time. Two of his shots were probably misses, for he heard no response, but the third one must have scored. He heard a yell, broken off at its zenith, and got an impression of faltering motion, as though a figure was struggling to stay on its feet. Then he heard a heavy thud and picked out a dark blob lying against the ground. The man's breathing was heavy and he was sobbing as he struggled for another breath of air. Then that sound was silenced, and only stillness pressed down on the scene.

Bud waited a moment longer. "You all right, Billy?" he hissed.

"Scared to death," came the response. "They didn't hit me. You all right, Marshal?"

"All right," Bud answered in a shaky whisper.

"They came close, didn't they?"

"Too damned close."

"Who was it?"

"I haven't seen them. I'm guessing it was the Mallorys."

"You think it's over?"

"I think so. They're both down."

"Then why are we whispering?"

Bud grinned. This kid went straight to the heart of the matter. "Damned if I know."

Startled cries sounded in the distance, and Bud heard the pound of running feet. "I think you can get up now, Billy," he said, still holding the gun, ready to use it at the faintest stirring of life from the two bodies.

"I think you got them, Marshal."

Bud put the gun away and dusted himself off. "I think so too, Billy."

The cries were much closer now, coming from behind and ahead of them. The shots must have aroused half of the town. On second thought, Bud drew the gun again. This was a raw, rough community, and its emotions were unpredictable. Anybody wearing a badge had been disliked before, and that dislike could easily extend to him, particularly on top of another shooting.

"What's all that shooting about?" somebody called querulously.

"Over here," Bud called. "Come in damned easy. There's been a gun fight."

Bud judged fifty men crowded around him and Billy. Two of them carried torches, and the breeze stirred the flames into wavering light. It put menacing shadows on faces and seemed to tighten them. Their animosity was as tangible as a slap in the face. Were these people aware of this ambush? The thought flashed through Bud's mind. They seemed to get here damned quick. Perhaps they hoped to see Bud stretched out on the ground.

Bud growled at himself for the unfounded suspicion. The shots were enough to draw them, and he couldn't see anything abnormal in their reactions. No, none of these men were actually involved in the attack.

"It's that damned marshal," somebody growled. "Who were you firing at?"

Bud grinned tight-lipped at them. After his run-in with Lem, he couldn't expect to be popular. This double shooting would only heighten that dislike.

"A couple of bushwhackers," Bud answered.

"Who were they?"

Bud shook his head. "I don't know. I haven't looked at them. One of them is on this side of the street, the other's over there."

The crowd split, half of it going to Bud's right, the other half going to the left.

The torches were held close over the bodies. "Jesus," a man said in surprise. "This one is Jonse."

"Deke's over here," a man called from across the street. "The darn fools. They were so hot to get the marshal, they didn't use their heads. Hell, if Lem couldn't do it, they sure couldn't."

"They should have," an argumentative voice stated. "There were two of them."

"But they didn't," came a stiff answer. "You're looking at the proof."

They came back to Bud and Billy, curiosity growing in their voices. "How'd it start, Marshal?"

Bud thought the animosity had faded a little in the question. They lived a rough life in a rough town. The only thing they respected was power, regardless of how it was displayed.

"Tell them, Billy," Bud said.

The confidence in Billy's voice showed how much he was enjoying his new importance. "We'd been out all afternoon. We left our mounts at the livery stable and were headed for Ma Atkin's restaurant. You know it's the only fit place to eat." He paused, and his broad grin flashed. He was the center of attention, and he was going to milk the moment to its last drop.

"Go on," somebody yelled at him.

Billy stared indignantly at the speaker, then resumed his narration. "The marshal saw movement on that side of the street." He pointed to his right. "The marshal's smart. He knew what was coming. He pushed me off my feet, then dove for the ground." He paused to rub his elbow in reflection of that dreadful moment.

"Will you get on with it?" an unhappy listener yelled.

"That's when the first shot came, but the marshal was rolling, and it missed him by a good three feet. He dropped that bushwhacker with a single shot." His eyes were gleaming. "God, you should've heard him squeal. It must have drove the other brother crazy, for he stepped out of his hiding place and cut loose a shot at the marshal. The marshal fired three shots in return, and I heard the same loud scream. Then everything was quiet—until you people came up yelling your darn fool questions."

Billy winked at Bud. He was well pleased with himself.

Bud forgave him for showing off. Billy had told the story fairly accurately, and it would keep all those curious questions from being directed at him.

"You did a job, Marshal," a man in the crowd said grudgingly. "None of the Mallorys was much good. Nobody's going to do much crying over them."

"I'm not," Bud said crisply. This was a chance to drive home an object lesson, and he couldn't let it pass. "If anybody in this town is planning on trying a similar action, I hope they remember this night."

They got his point, for all through the crowd heads bobbed. "They'd sure be crazy to go ahead with such plans," a man nearest Bud muttered.

Bud nodded. At least he had earned some respect, and he would rather it be earned through friendship rather than the brutal hand of violence. But he would take it any way he could.

"Somebody see that those bodies are picked up. Let's go, Billy." He placed an arm about the kid's shoulders and walked down the street with him.

"You sure showed them," Billy crowed.

"I'd rather it was some other way," Bud said soberly. "Do you think anybody in that crowd likes me?"

"They might not like you," Billy admitted, "but they sure as hell ain't going to try to push you around anymore."

"Well, that's something," Bud said, and sighed. Lord, he was suddenly weary. It was odd how much just a few violent moments could take out of a man.

"Were you really scared, Billy?" Bud asked.

"No," Billy started, then gulped. "That's not true," he confessed. "It happened too fast for me to get really scared. But after it was all over was when I started being scared. I thought for sure you'd hear my teeth chattering."

Bud smiled at him. This was a tough, honest kid. Bud doubted that anybody in that crowd was aware that fear had ever touched Billy. If Billy kept on at this rate, he was going to grow up into a competent man.

"Were you scared, Marshal?"

"Like you said, Billy, it happened and built up too fast to even think of being scared. But afterward I had a few sober thoughts about what had just occurred. The Mallorys were a little too eager. If they had waited a few seconds longer, it might have turned out differently."

"It sure could have," Billy said, and shook his head. "I'll bet you one thing."

"What's that, Billy?"

"Nobody in this town will ever risk the crazy stunt of trying to get you again."

Bud laughed wryly. "I sure hope you're right. Let's go get something to eat."

"You hungry?" Billy asked curiously.

"Not as hungry as before that ruckus started, but once we see food I think our appetites will return."

Bud hoped so. This day wasn't over yet. He had a long report to write to Nix. Three dead men in two nights—he was running up a score in a hurry. He wouldn't want Nix to think he had hired a gun-crazy kid. After he explained all that, he had to write about the horses stolen from Kaiser. He had to tell Nix about the tattoos on the horses' lips and explain his hunch that the animals might have been driven into Texas. He was also going to ask Nix to use his influence with the Rangers.

Bud sighed. It was going to be a long letter, and he wasn't too happy at the prospect. He and letter writing had never been close. Well, it would be worth it if he could replace the contempt with respect in Kaiser's eyes. It could be done. Hadn't he earned a grudging respect from the townspeople tonight? But finding those horses was going to be much more difficult, he warned himself.

Chapter 10

"Have enough?" Bud asked Billy as they left the restaurant.

"If I ate any more, I'd have busted," Billy answered. "What do we do now?"

"I've got some reports to get ready. I'll be tied up for quite a while."

Billy grinned wisely. "In other words, get lost."

Bud chuckled. "You're too smart for your own good. You can hang around the office if you want to, but don't interrupt me."

Billy considered what Bud said. "You'd be just as pleased if I took off." He held up a hand at the distress creeping into Bud's face. "It's time I got home, anyway. Pa will be wondering what became of me. Should I come in tomorrow, Bud?"

"Why not?"

"The cleaning's all done. I don't know if I still have a job."

Bud was annoyed and amused. The only thing wrong about this kid was his flip tongue. He said anything that popped into his mind. "I'll tell you when you're through," he said gruffly. "Until then, consider yourself still working. Good night, Billy."

Billy raised a hand and sauntered down the street. Bud watched him until he was out of sight, then unlocked his office door and stepped inside. He lit the lamp, and the shadows crept away from its reaching radiance. The place looked pretty good, if he did say so himself. He sat down at the desk and pulled several pieces of paper out of the top drawer. He frowned at the supply remaining. He'd have to tell Crump he needed stationery.

He picked up a pencil, and the point was blunted. He scowled at it. Every aggravation that could happen usually did when he struggled to write a letter. He pulled out his knife, opened a blade, and carefully sharpened the pencil, letting the shavings fall into the wastebasket. After several false starts, Bud cursed and threw the sheet into the wastebasket too. He should know he couldn't finish the letter with his first sheet of paper. He wanted a powerful sentence, one that would catch Nix's attention and hold it.

"Ah," he said, with satisfaction as the sentence formed in his mind: "I killed a man on my first day in Chandler." The start seemed to unlock the block to his thoughts and they flowed easily. "I found out later he was one of the bully boys, holding the town in a reign of terror. I saw from the start that he was primed for trouble, but he wouldn't listen to reason. I told him to go ahead, and he drew. His reputation said he was fast, but the reputation was false. His name was Lem Mallory."

Bud paused, reading what he had written. He would bet Nix wouldn't put this letter down.

"The second night, I killed two more men, brothers of Lem Mallory. They tried to ambush me, but they were clumsy. Both of them fired first, only their aim was bad and I was lucky enough to get them both. I do think this harsh example will have a calming effect on the town.

"But another thing is bothering me. Old man Kaiser came in to report the theft of twenty of his thoroughbred horses. The only trouble is that it happened six weeks ago. I think Kaiser reported it to me out of a vindictive curiosity to see what the law would do. I rode out to his place, but there were no tracks, no leads of any kind. I did learn an interesting piece of information, though. All thoroughbred horses are tattooed on the inside of the upper lip. I never heard of it before, and I bet the thief didn't either.

"I've got a strong hunch those horses might have been driven into Texas. Do you have any standing with the Texas Rangers? If so, could you ask them to keep an eye open for those tattoos? If I can find out where the horses were sold, I might be able to track them. I've got a strong feeling the thieves came from around here. It would sure be a big help if you could find out anything. Put all the pressure you can on the Rangers. I'll be chewing my lip until I hear from you."

Bud leaned back in his chair as he read what he had written. He knew he wasn't the best writer in the world, but this didn't sound so bad. He would have to wait for Nix's reply, and that would be the hardest part. What if Nix didn't answer promptly? He could think it was a greenhorn trying to press higher authority and shrug it off. Nix hadn't better do that, Bud thought grimly. He'd bombard him with letters until the sheer weight of them would make him change his mind.

It was fairly early in the evening, and he didn't want to go back to that lonely room. Lilah, he thought, and was aware of the accelerated beat of his heart. He walked over to the saloon, and the usual rowdy crowd was present. For a moment they didn't notice him, then the blast of talk and laughter subsided until it was only a faint echo. He nodded to the watching men, not expecting a warm response. He wasn't exactly liked yet, but he thought there was more respect in the glances they gave him.

As he walked up to the bar, one man said, "Howdy, Marshal."

It was a small thing, but Bud gave him a grateful glance. "And to you," Bud replied. He was smiling as he leaned against the bar.

Lilah gave him a frosty flash of her eyes. This was going to be the hardest piece of ice to shatter. "You look pleased with yourself," she said crisply. "Any particular reason?"

"I'm alive," he returned. "A man just spoke to me. That's a gain."

Lilah eyed him curiously, then shook her head. "I can't figure you out," she remarked.

Bud's teeth flashed. "I'm just a simple man."

"What'll you have?" she asked crossly, as though displeased by the trend the conversation had taken.

"The usual," he answered.

She drew a glass of beer, and there was deftness and care in the way she served him. "You're making a big name for yourself," she said. The sharpness was still in her voice.

"How's that?" he asked, though he knew what she meant.

"How many men do you figure you have to kill to make your reputation?"

A faint wince touched Bud's face. He expected that. It would be on every tongue for several days.

"You think that's what I'm doing?"

"Isn't it?" she challenged.

"Hardly," he said brusquely. "Do you think I enjoy killing men?"

She wouldn't meet his direct gaze. "It's beginning to look like it," she said, her tone cold.

"I don't know what you heard, but you've got it all twisted. I didn't seek out those two. They were waiting for me. They weren't very good at it, and they missed. It came down to them or me," His face twisted. "I think you know what I'll pick every time."

Lilah was beginning to be flustered under those probing eyes. "I know how it looks to me. Three killings in such a short time. It makes me wonder."

"Those killings were forced on me," Bud said heatedly. "You saw how it happened with Lem. His brothers followed the same road." His hope of having an easier relationship with her was fading. She didn't like the killings, and she was telling him so. "It's my job. I was sent down here to jerk this town back into line. If it took the Mallorys—" He shrugged. "Then that's the way it has to be."

"So you're the angel appointed to hover over Chandler."

Bud was smarting under her vicious riding. "If it looks that way, I can't do anything about it. I want to rid Chandler of all its lawbreakers."

"With a gun?" she jeered.

"If it has to be that way," he said levelly. "Today I heard of another kind of lawbreaker, a low-down horse thief."

"Who told you that?" Her voice had a new sharpness.

"Old man Kaiser. He lost twenty good horses."

"And you promised you'd recover them for him?"

"I didn't promise him anything, but I think I can do it. Why in the hell are you getting so stiff-necked? If I can run the lawbreakers out of town, it will be a better place to live."

She recoiled before the blaze in his eyes. Perhaps she had pushed this too far. "Getting rid of that kind doesn't bother me. It's just your way of going about it."

Bud pushed back his half-finished beer. "I'm sorry my way displeases you. I've gone too far to change." He nodded curtly and walked to the door. He looked back, and she was watching him. He knew a sickening sense of loss. Something could have built up between them. He knew it. Things could have been so different.

Lilah turned the bar over to her floorman. He was thoroughly reliable and could be trusted with the cash flow. "Butch, I'll be back in a little while."

A little smirk started in his eyes. He guessed where she was going. She stared coldly at him, and the smirk slowly faded. Butch knew Lilah's temper. Upset her too much, and he could be out on his ear.

Lilah walked out and climbed the outside stairs to her rooms over the saloon. She shivered as she remembered the marshal's level, burning eyes. She had to get word to Toby to be more careful than ever. The marshal was a deadly man with a drive that would carry him to whatever he wanted to accomplish.

A faint curiosity stirred within her. Could she have bent the marshal to her purpose? A woman's intuition told her that she could. Oh, she couldn't change him into someone unlawful, but she could soften and blind him. Right now, however, he was extremely dangerous to her. She wouldn't be able to breathe freely until she had thoroughly obscured all traces of her participation in the ring that had stolen so many horses.

Lilah opened the door and stepped into the room. Toby lounged in a chair, his shirt off, a bottle of beer in his hand.

"What are you doing here?"

"Hi, baby," he said. "I couldn't stay away from you any longer."

A little twinge of disgust ran through her. "I asked you a question," she said sharply.

"That Grimes' place bored me. I couldn't stand it any longer." He stared plaintively at her. "Lilah, it's been so long. Don't you ever feel loneliness?"

"Toby, did you hear the marshal killed two more men tonight?"

"I heard," he said lazily. "He's a lucky bum."

"Maybe not so lucky," she said quietly. "They set up an ambush for him and missed. He got both of them. And you think he's lucky," she finished bitterly.

Nothing Lilah said bothered Toby. "Jonse and Deke weren't too bright. They didn't have enough sense to trap a chicken."

Her bitterness increased. "You would have handled it differently?"

"You can bet on that. I wouldn't be lying out there dead," he said complacently.

Lilah wanted to scream. Toby was a vain, egotistical man. "You better never get such a thought in your head," she lashed out at him. "If the marshal even thought you were thinking such things, he'd come after you. By now you've seen or heard enough of his ability with a gun. A smart man would shrink back if the marshal ever looked his way."

That stung Toby. "You think I'm not bright enough to take care of myself?"

God, how he infuriated her. She could have pointed out that he wasn't taking care of himself now. She could lay hard, solid facts before him and he wouldn't even blink.

"Toby, I told you to lay low for a while. I don't want anybody seeing you coming to this room."

He gaped at her. "Why?" he demanded.

"Because the marshal is looking for the one who stole Kaiser's horses."

Toby laughed in genuine delight. "Let him look all he wants to. That was over six weeks ago. We took them away clean—didn't leave a track. If we had, the rains would have washed them away." He laughed again.

The sound scraped on Lilah's nerves. "Shut up, you damned fool," she screamed at him. "This marshal is smart. He comes up with whatever he goes after. Nothing he does surprises me."

That stopped his laughter, and his eyes narrowed. "Sounds to me like you might be falling for him."

"That's ridiculous," she said furiously. "I'm only thinking of you. I want you to get away while the getting is good."

Toby's face was pinched with suspicion. "You better hope he doesn't run those horses down. You're in this, too. You thought of the horses at Kaiser's."

She managed to make her laughter sound natural. "Toby, do you realize we're quarreling? What's that old saying? Thieves always fall out."

Toby wasn't mollified. "That's not funny," he growled.

Lilah threw up her hands in mock despair. "Don't you see that I'm only thinking about you? I want you away until this furor about the horses dies down, which it will," she assured him. "There's no trail. The marshal's good but not good enough to find something where nothing exists."

Toby still peered suspiciously at her. "I wish I knew what's in your head," he complained. "I still think he's caught your eye."

Lilah moved over to him and sat down on his lap. She kissed him long and hard. The reek of beer was strong on his breath, but she let the kiss last until Toby broke it. She caught her breath and asked, "Does that convince you?"

"Almost," he said, and grinned. He tried to pull her back to him, and she resisted.

"Toby, I want you to get out of town and stay out. Now, while you can." She grabbed his beard and shook his head. "Do you think I want anything happening to you?"

"You're sure?" he demanded.

She sighed with exasperation. Toby had an animal's streak of suspicion. "I'm sure. You lay low until I'm sure all trace of danger is gone."

"If I leave, how can I keep in touch with you?" he complained.

"I'll keep in touch with you."

He pulled at her again, and she went into his arms. She didn't want his damned beer-reeking kisses, but this would be a cheap price to be temporarily rid of him. Finally, she braced both her hands against his chest and pushed hard. "Toby, I think you should leave now."

"All right," he said reluctantly. His eyes were veiled, and she couldn't read them. "But, by God, you better keep in touch with me."

She lightly brushed his lips with her mouth. "Oh, I will," she promised.

Chapter 11

Ten days passed before Bud heard from Nix. His cussing grew more intense with each passing day. The letter he thought would stir Nix into action apparently had no effect.

He ripped open the envelope with impatient fingers, and read it eagerly: "Your letter was interesting. Glad to hear you think you have the town under control. In some spots, a gun seems to be the only answer. I put off answering your letter because I was trying to arrange matters so that I could go down to Texas. Amarillo's holding a wanted criminal, and I wanted to go down to bring him back. Until your letter came, it was all set up for another officer to go, but when I read what you had written, I saw a chance to kill two birds with one stone. It took a couple of days to change the plans. I'll talk to the Rangers about the tattooed horses. Don't get impatient. It'll take some time for the Rangers to nose around. I'll write as soon as I know anything."

Bud's fingernails dug into his palm in frustration. God, how he wanted to show two people. He wanted to wipe out the derision in Kaiser's eyes and erase the contempt in Lilah's face. He rose and strode around the desk. Damn, he was getting restless. He hadn't done much since the night of the ambush. Oh, he made his hourly rounds, but the town was unusually quiet. Perhaps Nix was right when he said the quickest way to control a town was with a gun.

He missed stopping in at Lilah's saloon. He had tried a couple of others, and they were inferior in furnishings and the quality of the beer they served. Would that same dislike show on her face, if he went back? It probably would, he concluded. Anyway, he wasn't going to risk it again.

He whirled at the scrape of footsteps in the doorway. His scowl relaxed at the sight of Billy. He knew he was jumpy to start at any normal sound, but this town was a long way from being tamed.

Billy was accompanied by a big man with stooped shoulders. Huge hands hung at the end of massive arms, and he moved slowly, as though he was nearing exhaustion. By the looks of him, this man had known the seamier aspects of life. His clothes were well worn, almost shabby, and his face was lined.

"Marshal," Billy said, "I want you to meet my pa. Elmer, this is the man I've talked so much about."

Elmer thrust out a massive paw, and it swallowed Bud's hand. This man didn't know the full extent of his power, and Bud managed to keep his face composed as the big hand squeezed his.

"I'm sure glad to meet you," Elmer rumbled. "I wanted to thank you for giving Billy a job. You've done a lot for him."

"He's already done a lot for me," Bud said gravely. "He might have saved my life by pointing out and warning me about the Mallory boys."

"Aw," Billy grumbled.

"Billy doesn't like being praised," Elmer said, and chuckled. "He's always been a modest kid."

"A good quality," Bud said. "But when a man does something that merits praise, I say he's entitled to hear it."

"You hear that, Billy?" Elmer asked, and his booming laughter filled the room. "I'm obliged to you, Marshal, for setting Billy an example. When he sees what can happen to the lawbreakers, I think it'll keep his head straight. You've certainly made a big change so far in this town."

"I intend to keep it that way," Bud said quietly. "Billy tell you about our visit to Kaiser's farm?"

Elmer bobbed his head. "He sure did. He said something about twenty horses being lifted right out of the old man's pasture. You think you'll ever find those horses?"

"I'm looking for them," Bud said broodingly. "It happened over six weeks ago. I'm getting a real late start."

Elmer nodded in sympathy. "Almost the same thing happened to me." His face had grown grim. "Over a year ago. I had a pretty fair start, a little piece of ground and a dozen mares. I spent more money than I should have, but I wanted to improve the future colts." His face twisted at recounting something that was very painful. "Borrowed money from the bank." His shoulders lifted and fell. "Those rotten horse thieves stole the mares and the stallion."

"Never found a trace of them? Weren't they branded?"

"I wore myself out trying to find them," Elmer said despondently. "The bank foreclosed on me when I couldn't make the payments. There went my place. Sure, those horses were branded, but that won't stop a clever horse thief. He can alter those brands until the original owner couldn't recognize his own horses if he stared them in the eye." His big hand closed, making the knuckles stand out prominently. "I'd sure like to run across that bunch of scum."

Bud's interest sharpened. In one way, he was better off than Elmer. The thieves couldn't do much with hidden tattoos. "Elmer, do you think there's an organized ring operating around here?"

"I know it," Elmer said emphatically. "Too much horse stealing going on. Hell, there's reports of new losses every few weeks."

"You have the slightest idea of who they might be?"

A curse rumbled in Elmer's throat. "Not the slightest. Damn it, if I had one, don't you think I'd be after them?"

"I guess so," Bud said wryly. He started to tell Elmer about the tattoos, then decided against it. Not that he couldn't trust Elmer, but the fewer who had this information, the better.

"Took enough of your time, Marshal," Elmer said. "I'm happy to have met you."

"My pleasure, Elmer." Bud steeled himself to meet the awesome power in that massive hand and thrust out his own.

"Appreciate what you've done for Billy," Elmer said gravely. "If he doesn't do what you tell him, whop him. You've got my permission."

Bud shook his head. "Can't see a time when something like that would be necessary. You've raised a good boy, Elmer."

"You don't know how good that sounds to me." Elmer lightly punched Billy on the biceps. "Ready to go home, son?"

"Ready, Pa. Thanks, Marshal, for everything."

Bud brushed aside the words. "Don't know what you're talking about." But he did know. Billy was grateful that he had taken time to talk to his father and for the way he treated him.

"Elmer," he said, checking the big man. "You hear anything about those horse thieves, you let me know."

"You can bet on it," Elmer replied.

Bud remained motionless until they left. Every now and then, an honest person appeared in this miserable town. He was grateful to Billy for bringing his father by, and he was grateful to Elmer for the conversation. It filled out his information about what was going on around Chandler, and it had filled up some of the time.

Bud locked the office door behind him and walked down the street. Two men passed, and both of them said, "Howdy, Marshal."

"Howdy," he returned. Things had improved. Not too long ago, nobody had spoken to him. It was faint recognition, but it was an improvement.

He stopped just inside the door of the saloon, his eyes going to Lilah. She was busy as usual, but she saw him come in. She stared at him a moment, and faint, rosy color suffused her face.

He couldn't believe it. A smile was stealing across her

face. Bud crossed to the bar, and Lilah came up immediately.

"Hello," she said gravely.

He noticed the rapid beating of the pulse at the base of her throat. "Hello," he returned soberly.

"The same?" she asked.

"The same," he replied.

Lilah drew the beer and set it carefully before him. For a moment, a silence gripped both of them. He wondered if she was having as much trouble finding the right words as he was.

"I thought you'd deserted us," she said, trying to keep her voice light.

Bud smiled. "I thought you didn't want me to come back."

She gave him a full view of those magnificent eyes before she lowered them. "You didn't think that," she protested, making it sound as though that was too awful to contemplate.

Bud nodded gravely. "Yes, I did—so much so that I punished myself with an inferior brand of beer. I thought I'd come back once more to find out if I could stay, or if you'd have me thrown out."

She giggled, a light, pleased burst of sound. "Who would I get to do that? My floorman? The customers? Everybody in here knows you. Do you think any of them would be foolish enough to try that?"

Bud chuckled. He felt at ease. The conversation was going far differently than he feared. "I hope not. I'm sorry I made you so unhappy when I had to shoot the Mallory brothers, but—"

She cut him short. "You were only doing your job. There was no way of avoiding that. Even when I seemed the most distressed"—those expressive shoulders moved in a small shrug—"it was just the thought of all that bloodshed."

He didn't blame her at all for feeling that way. It was only that warm, sensitive streak expressing itself. "Do you think I liked doing that?" he asked.

"I know you didn't," she said in a subdued voice. "Can't we forget about that and just be friends?"

He enclosed her small hand in his. "I'd like nothing better," he said sincerely.

He held the hand as long as he dared. It was the first time he had ever touched her, and the feel of the warm, vibrant flesh sent a series of pulsing tingles through him. He could think now that his stay in Chandler had turned toward the pleasant side, and that wasn't imagination. He saw that in those beautiful eyes. From now on, she would not try to avoid him.

Chapter 12

The next two weeks were the happiest Bud had known since he was a kid. He saw Lilah every night, and they dined together three or four times a week. When she thought she could leave the bar, they walked together. She regretfully turned down a buggy ride, for that would keep her away from her work too late.

He had never kissed her, but last night she had brushed his cheek with her lips. He swore he could still feel the pressure of her lips the next day. He had lain awake far into the night, the heady aroma of the perfume she wore still with him. If it hadn't been for the other sleeping boarders, he would have whooped with his delight. Lord, he was serious about this woman!

Did she feel the same about him? He wrestled with that question for a long while, and it was a tough adversary. Damn it, she had to be, or she wouldn't have kept on seeing him. He shook his head. In just those two weeks, he had made tremendous progress with her. He would ask her a direct question tomorrow night.

He raised his hands and looked at them. They were shaking. What if she refused him? He groaned in agony at the thought. Maybe he would be wiser not to rush things so fast. No, he would approach her a cautious step at a time, letting her reactions to him build up his confidence.

He rolled over, satisfied with the solution he had chosen.

Chandler was no longer a miserable town to him. It had a newfound glow, and Lilah was the sole cause of it.

Bud was getting drowsy when a stabbing thought made him sit bolt upright. What if Nix decided his job was done here and transferred him to another district? He groaned at the thought. Nix couldn't do that; he wouldn't let him. Hell, his job here wasn't done. He hadn't begun to unravel the horse stealing. That thought widened his eyes. Lilah had so befuddled his thinking that he had forgotten all about expecting a letter from Nix. He swore at Nix before he settled down again. Nix had had more than enough time to answer. Did he think Bud was just playing with some toy?

He was hollow-eyed in the morning; all of those troubled thoughts had played hell with his sleep. He walked into the office, and Billy came in a moment later.

"I stopped by the post office," Billy said, handing over a couple of letters. The first piece was an ad, and Bud threw it into the wastebasket. His heart picked up a beat at the sight of the familiar writing on the second envelope. Nix had finally answered.

"Sorry to have delayed so long, Bud," he read. "My prisoner made a break for it just before I arrived and almost succeeded. It took a couple of extra days to find him. But I got him back. He won't break out of the jail here."

Bud nodded absently. Losing that prisoner would have stung Nix. He was proud of his reputation, and when he went after a man he brought him back.

Bud's eyes shifted impatiently. Had he found out anything about those tattooed horses?

"I talked to Dusty Rhodes," Nix continued, "a Ranger sergeant at Amarillo. Dusty knew all about horses being tattooed like that. He says it might take a little time to locate them, if they are in this country, but he'll put men on it. I gave him your name and address. When and if he gets hold of anything, he'll notify you. He sent a few cuss words your way. You didn't send him much to go on."

Bud winced. He couldn't argue against the validity of that accusation. Now he had to wait until he heard from

Rhodes. He hadn't the slightest idea of how long that would take. It could be never.

Billy was watching him curiously. "Any important news?"

"What makes you ask that?" Bud asked crossly.

"The way your face worked."

Bud laughed shortly. "Did it show that much?"

"Sure did. You'd make a hell of a poor poker player."

"I won't be sitting across the table from you." Bud smiled to take the sting out of the rebuke. "It wasn't bad news, but not good, either."

He tucked the letter back into its envelope and locked it in the top desk drawer. He wrote a brief letter to Nix acknowledging the information he had sent, sealed it, and handed it to Billy. "Run this down to the post office, will you?"

"Sure." Billy seized the letter and was off on a dead run.

Bud heard a startled ejaculation at the door, and a grumpy voice yelled, "Damn it, watch where you're going! You almost ran me down."

Bud sighed. That was Crump's unhappy voice, and he wondered what the old coot had to complain about today.

Crump came in and walked to the desk. "That kid almost ran me down! Is he worth the money you're paying him? What's he doing now?"

"Running a letter to the post office. I think he's worth every cent he gets." He didn't pay Billy much, but Crump, with his picky mind, criticized every spent penny that came to his attention.

"Well, I don't," Crump snapped. "That's how a town's expenses get away from the officials elected to control spending. They close their eyes to the spending of a dollar here and a dollar there. Before you know it, the town is broke. It's not going to happen under my administration."

Bud sighed. Crump was in a foul mood today, more so than usual. He might as well endure it.

Crump looked around, his face pinched. "Where am I supposed to sit?"

Bud sat in the only chair in the office. "On the corner of the desk," he retorted.

"Hell of a note. One chair in an office. Do you expect a visitor to stand?"

"I do," Bud snapped, "until you supply more chairs."

"Don't need them." Crump quickly closed the subject.

Bud wondered why he was here. Certainly not to complain about minor expenses, though that was his favorite subject.

"What's on your mind, Mayor?" he asked curtly.

"Been wanting to talk about this for some time." Crump's eyes wouldn't meet Bud's. "Passing by here this morning and decided it might as well be now as later." He paused and looked at the floor.

The silence grew long, and Bud said impatiently, "Get on with it."

"You're an official of the town, ain't you?" This time, Crump looked at Bud with judging eyes, tapping his teeth with a forefinger.

Good Lord, Bud thought impatiently, what in the hell is he driving at? "I guess you could consider me as one."

"Then I think your behavior should be more prudent—an example to the citizens of Chandler."

Bud leaned forward, his face set. "You're going to have to put it plainer."

Crump's eyes shifted. His mouth was a tight, pinched line. "You've been seen with that woman too often for your own good."

Bud felt as though the breath had been kicked out of him. This old fool was talking about Lilah. He was furious and unhappy, and he had to be careful of what he said, or else he would be cursing Crump out.

"That's none of your business," he said through clenched teeth.

A hot flush spread across Crump's face. "I think it is, when it concerns the town's welfare. She can do you a lot of harm, though you may be too young to realize it."

Bud was raging inwardly. He leaned back in his chair, seeking a semblance of control over himself. "Who's been giving you reports?" he demanded.

"A lot of people have seen you," Crump replied shrilly. "I've seen you myself several times. Taking her out to supper and all that sort of foolish nonsense." He seemed to be having trouble with his breathing, for he panted. "I'm telling you it's got to stop."

Bud gripped the edge of the desk, his knuckles standing out starkly. Another moment of this, and he was going to pitch Crump out. "Leave it alone," he warned. "I told you before it's none of your business."

Crump's face was congested. "Damn it, Bud, I'm only thinking of your own good. Anything bad happening to you will reflect on the town, because as I've told you, you're an important official." A pleading note crept into his voice. "Can't you see she's no good for you? She's a lot older. She can do a lot of harm."

That tore it right down the middle. Bud got up from the chair, advanced around the desk, and seized Crump's shirt with both hands. He thrust his face close to Crump's and said furiously, "I told you to leave it alone. If you keep on, I'll throw you out of here."

Crump was thoroughly frightened, for his voice squeaked. "You can't talk to me like this. I can fire you."

Crump couldn't fire him, not with Nix behind him. Crump would have to get Nix's consent to even have Bud recalled.

"Keep on," Bud growled, and gathered more of the shirt material in his hands.

Crump had some courage. Even looking into those furious eyes, he added a few more things: "Bud, you're young. You haven't had enough experience with that kind of woman. She's using you. Ever since I've known her, she's run a wild place. Maybe I can't prove it, but a lot of odd things have come out of that saloon. I'm telling you—"

"You've just run out of time," Bud said angrily. He spun Crump around and propelled him to the door. He gave a final shove, and the force sent Crump flying. He wound up sprawling in the street.

Bud coldly looked down at him. "Don't come back here."

Crump struggled to a sitting position. He screamed obscenities and shook both fists. "You haven't heard the last of this," he howled. "I've got some authority. I'll use it."

The threat didn't touch Bud. Perhaps he should have been alarmed, but he wasn't. There was nothing frightening about that figure sitting in the dust. He was only pitiful. Bud turned and slammed the door against the torrent of expletives.

Four days later, Crump's denunciation had only set Bud's mind more firmly. He was going to see Lilah whenever he chose, if she was willing. He had met her every night since Crump's visit, but that old man had ruined something for him.

This evening, he had glanced about constantly to see if anybody was watching them surreptitiously. They had almost reached the outdoor stairs of her saloon when Lilah asked, "What's troubling you, Bud?"

"Nothing," he said hastily. He didn't want to tell her about Crump for fear it might put a damper on their relationship. He knew it had for him.

"Yes, there is," she insisted. "Don't you think I can tell?"

Bud sighed. Maybe she could. It might be wiser for him to blurt out what was troubling him.

He took a deep breath. "Lilah, you're right. Something is bothering me. Old man Crump stopped by the other day. He said some things that made me pitch him out."

"Ah," she said tonelessly. "He came by to tell you how bad it is for you to be seen with me."

He looked at her in amazement. "How did you know?"

"I knew it was inevitable," she said quietly. "Since we've been seeing each other, I knew it wouldn't take long for some nosy person to run to Crump and tell him."

Bud's amazement didn't lessen. She sounded as though she had been there and heard the conversation.

She laid a hand on his forearm. "Don't worry about it, Bud. There's a lot of people who are unhappy at seeing others happy. They can't rest until they destroy that happiness. Mayor Crump warned you I could be harmful to you?"

Bud nodded solemnly. "That's why I pitched him out."

"He won't forgive you for that," she said slowly. "He is a vindictive old man. I know."

She looked so troubled he wanted to take her into his arms and comfort her. "Do you want to tell me about it?"

She managed a strained smile. "It all sounds so foolish." Her eyes searched his face, and she sighed. "I want you to know about it. He used to pester me to see him." Her voice almost broke off, and Bud nodded. He knew exactly how she felt.

"I tried to tell him no, gently," she went on, "but he wouldn't listen. He kept at it until I couldn't stand it any longer. I finally told him in a way that even his thick head could understand. I've never seen a man so angry. He swore I'd be sorry, that I'd regret turning him down." She tried to smile, and it was a ghastly effort. "He was so right."

"What did he do?" Bud exploded.

"Just little, sly tricks. He saw that my taxes were raised. He confronted me with every city ordinance he could. He made it as difficult as possible for me to get deliveries. Somebody from the council constantly inspects my place to see if I'm violating some law."

"That miserable, old son-of-a—" Bud said savagely. "When I get through talking to him, things will change."

"Don't do it, Bud," she begged. "Can't you see that it'll only make things worse. He'll find new ways to apply more pressure on me."

"No, he won't," Bud said stubbornly. "Not when I get through with him. I'll—"

Her hand rose to stroke his cheek. "Please, Bud. Just leave it as it is. You don't know how tough I am. I'll survive."

She no longer touched his cheek, but he could still feel the soft touch of those fingers. "Lilah, do you like me?"

She stared at him, perplexed. "You know I do. Why do you think I've been seeing you."

His heart bounded in joy. Her answer had given him

the confidence he needed. "I asked you that because I've got a more important question to ask." He drew her into his arms, and she didn't resist. "Marry me, Lilah." He kissed her and the response of her lips was all the answer he would ever need. He raised his head and said huskily, "As my wife, Crump won't dare do anything to annoy you."

She snuggled more closely to him. "That could be the solution," she murmured. "Oh, Bud, with you I'd feel safe."

He kissed her again. "Then your answer is yes?" He lightly shook her. "Don't keep me waiting too long, Lilah."

"Give me a little time, Bud," she pleaded. "I wasn't ready for this."

He laughed cheerfully. That was the typical feminine response. Women didn't like to be cornered. "As long as we're agreed on what we both want."

She brushed his lips with a light kiss. "I'll let you know soon."

He wanted to yell "make it tomorrow," but some sense of decorum held him. A girl would want a little time to herself. "You can't make it too soon for me," he said huskily.

She clasped his face between her hands and kissed him hard. "I think I want it that way, too." Wicked laughter filled her. It wasn't going to be hard to handle this impetuous, young man.

Bud remained rooted until Lilah climbed the stairs. She paused, turned, and blew him a kiss. He wanted to throw back his head and howl his joy. She had agreed to think about his proposal. He couldn't help but think of those wasted hours spent in worrying about her reaction. How wrong could a man get?

He beat his hands together in a quick flash of exuberance. Soon he would be a married man. He knew it with a conviction that couldn't be shaken. His face sobered. There wouldn't be too much time. He had a lot of things to do. He needed new clothes and new boots, then he must find a place for them to live. There were arrangements to be made for a preacher, and he didn't even know one.

All these little chores crowded in on him, and their weight almost scared him. Maybe he could ask Lilah to help him. She should know a preacher, and he might ask her to help him pick out his clothes. Was he suffering from an attack of pre-marital jitters? If so, he was going to crush them. He'd be damned if he'd let his nerves ruin what could be the most important day of his life.

Bud walked back to his boardinghouse, thought after thought crowding into his head. Thank God he had been careful with his pay; he had a small account in a bank in Guthrie. He would have to transfer that. Also, he should write Nix and tell him of his plans. Would Nix chuckle or frown at what Bud wrote him. Bud's jaw hardened. He didn't care how Nix or anybody else accepted what he was going to do. He was going to marry Lilah.

They had stayed out later than he thought, and he slipped quietly into Mrs. Edison's boardinghouse. He shook his head ruefully as he wondered how many people had seen them. Maybe Crump was one of them. It didn't matter.

He undressed and climbed into bed. He didn't give a damn what Crump said about his proposed plans. Just one disapproving word, and he would shut Crump up in a hurry.

Chapter 13

She's one day closer to me, Bud thought as he dressed. He went down for breakfast, and he didn't realize he was humming until Ames, one of the boarders, asked, "What makes you so happy?"

Bud smiled at him. "Just a lucky man I guess." Ames was a dour man with a jaundiced opinion of the world. Nothing could lift his spirits.

Bud never tasted food so good, and he complimented Mrs. Edison profusely.

"We must be eating two different kinds of food," Ames said querulously.

Bud grinned, but didn't comment. He wondered what had happened to Ames to turn him so sour.

He finished breakfast and went down to the office, half expecting to see Crump waiting for him. Instead, Billy was at the door.

"Morning Marshal. I beat you again," he crowed.

"You sure did," Bud agreed. He didn't want to get in a contest with this kid to see who could get to the office first. With Billy's eagerness, he'd have to come down at midnight.

"I stopped by the post office, Marshal." Bill was as dependable and responsible as anybody Bud had ever known.

"Any mail, Billy?"

Bud didn't look at the return address on the letter he

was handed until he opened the door and walked inside. He sat down and inspected the envelope. A stir of excitement ran through him. This letter was from Dusty Rhodes in Amarillo, Texas.

He slit it open, and there was a quiver in his fingers as he unfolded the single page. It was written on notebook paper in a large, uncontrolled scrawl. By the looks of the writing, Bud would say that writing wasn't one of Rhodes' particular pastimes.

"Hi, Marshal," he read. "Nix told me about your idea when he was down here. It was damned good. I never knew about it before. He told me to write you if I got any trace of the missing horses. Well, I've located eight of them. Broady bought them. He's never been too careful where he buys his stock. I got a chance to look at those upper lips. Every one of them was tattooed. Broady doesn't know anything about it yet. Thought you'd like to be down here when I move in on him. You'll want to be around when he tells me who he bought them horses from. Good luck, Dusty."

He locked the letter in the desk drawer.

"Must have been good news," Billy observed.

"What makes you say that?"

"The look on your face. It's shining like a new penny."

Bud grinned. "It's good news, Billy, but I'll have to be gone for a week or ten days." He caught the inquisitive gleam in the kid's eyes. "I'll tell you about it when I get back. Don't worry about your job. Your salary continues while I'm gone."

"I'd rather you be here," Billy said wistfully.

"I'll be back before you know it," Bud promised. The kid's face cleared. Bud hoped it would be as easy telling Crump and Lilah. Crump might raise a fuss, but he didn't have a solid base for an objection. Lilah could be difficult. After her promise to think his proposal over, here he was going away. Well, it had to be done.

Billy walked out of the office with him, and Bud said, "You stay out of trouble, Billy."

"I will," Billy promised. "Don't you worry. I'll keep an eye on things."

"Don't go poking into anything that's none of your business," Bud said sternly. "You just watch out for yourself." He rumpled Billy's hair. "That's the only important thing to me now."

"You mean that?" Billy's eyes were glowing.

"I mean that," Bud assured him, and continued down the street.

Bud found Crump just coming out of his house. "Mayor, I'm glad I caught you. I've got to be gone for a week or ten days. I'll get back as soon as I can."

Crump's eyes were narrowed and suspicious. "Does this proposed trip have anything to do with the town's business? Or has it to do with that woman?"

Bud gritted his teeth. "You leave Lilah out of this," he said coldly. "She has nothing to do with it."

"She had something to do with last night," Crump hissed. "You spent the whole evening with her."

If Crump hadn't seen them together, then somebody else in the town had. That news would get back to Crump as fast as the informer could move. "I told you to leave her out of this." Bud was getting angry.

"You're too young to know," Crump howled. "You don't have enough sense to realize when a woman is putting a ring in your nose. One of these days you'll realize she means you no good. Then it'll be too late."

That almost made Bud laugh. He called Crump hardheaded and Crump thought the same of him. The only difference between them was age. Bud could almost feel a pity for Crump. He had wanted Lilah badly enough to make a fool of himself.

Bud started to turn away. "I just wanted you to know that I'll be gone."

"You can't do that," Crump snapped. He was rapidly working himself into a rage. "Who's going to look after the town while you're gone? What if there's trouble?"

Bud gave him a taunting grin. "I'd say you better hope there's no trouble. Or you'll have to handle it yourself."

He walked away, not looking back. For several steps, he could hear Crump gasping and snorting. It sounded like the man was choking to death.

Lilah was just coming around the corner of her building to open up the saloon. "Bud," she cried. "You're here so early." Something struck her, for her eyes narrowed. "You didn't come to tell me you've changed your mind."

"Oh woman of little faith," he teased her. "You're the second person I've talked to this morning who suggested the same thing."

"Who was the other one?"

"The mayor," he replied. "He must have cared a lot for you. He's doing everything he can to make me change my mind."

Her eyes flashed, and she said heatedly, "I despise that man. I'd hurt him if I could think of a way."

Bud chuckled at this display of temper. "Pity him, Lilah. Most of his life's behind him. He regrets all he's missed. He needs pity more than anything else."

That calmed her down, for she said grudgingly, "Did you come by just to tell me that?"

"No," he replied. "I came by to tell you I have to leave town for a while. I'll be gone a week or ten days, but I'll be back as soon as I can."

Her face stiffened. "Are you thinking of changing your mind about us?"

He spread his hands eloquently. "Nothing could make me change my mind on that. It's official business, Lilah."

She sighed as she saw he wasn't going to say anything more. "I'm not as important to you as I thought I was."

She was indignant and half angry, and he tried to pacify her. "Not that at all, Lilah," he protested. "Something's come up that I have to attend to. Maybe my being gone will make you realize how much you need me."

Her tone was sulky. "I didn't think anything could come up that would make you push me aside."

"Stop that," he said sternly. "Lilah, I'll tell you all about it the moment I get back. Trust me. Right now, I can't tell you why I'm going."

She refused to be mollified. "You don't trust me enough to tell me why you're leaving."

He grabbed her upper arms. "You know better than that, Lilah. It looks like the trust is lacking on your part."

She melted all at once, falling against him. "I'm sorry," she whispered. "It's just that I'm so afraid of losing you."

She turned up a stricken face, and he kissed the proffered lips. He was no expert with women, but he guessed you had to be firm with them at times.

He lifted his head and said, "I'll get in touch with you the moment I get back. You can put that promise in the bank."

"It'll be a long wait, Bud." She smiled timorously. "But I'll manage."

He laughed. He had come over a sticky piece of ground without losing anything.

Chapter 14

Bud hadn't seen any part of Oklahoma that he would trade for Amarillo. The town was flat and high and the wind howled constantly. He had walked only a couple of blocks from the livery stable when he almost lost his hat to a sudden gust. At the intersection, he came up on a man who was waiting for a break in the traffic. His glance was friendly, and he confirmed the impression by saying, "Howdy."

"Howdy," Bud returned. "Does the wind always blow this hard?"

There was mild surprise in the man's eyes. "Blow?" he repeated, and shook his head. "Hell, this is a mild day. You should be here when it really cuts loose."

Bud grinned. "I'll pass, if you don't mind." Oklahoma had a reputation for windy weather, but if today was any sample of Amarillo's climate, Oklahoma couldn't hold a candle to it.

"Do you know where I can find Dusty Rhodes?" Bud asked.

"If he isn't in his office, I don't know where he is."

Bud chuckled. "Maybe that's my trouble. I don't know where his office is."

"Down the street a block." The man pointed out the direction. "A small office next to the barber shop."

"My thanks to you," Bud said.

The man made a disparaging motion. "For nothing." he scoffed. He made a cheery wave, then darted across the street between two big freight wagons.

Bud smiled after him. If he was an example of the people in Amarillo, a man couldn't help but like living here.

Bud found the office with no trouble. He peered in the door, and the man seated at the desk said, "Don't just stand there. Come in, come in."

He must have eyes in the back of his head, Bud thought, for he was seated with his back toward the door.

Bud entered, and the man swiveled to face him. "You Dusty?" Durable was the one word to describe him. He was as lean cut as a piece of whang leather and would last just about as long.

"That's me," the man acknowledged cheerfully. "You Carson?"

"How did you know that?"

"Been expecting you. Besides, anybody around here would know who I am without asking."

Bud had to know the answer to one more question. "How did you know I was standing at the door?"

Rhodes laughed. "You figure I have some special powers? Well, I haven't. Anybody walking along that board walk makes it sound like a drum. The pounding stopped, I figured you were looking in the door."

Bud shook his head in unconscious admiration. He would bet Rhodes was one hell of a law officer. "Remind me not to try and sneak up on you."

"I'll do that," Rhodes said and chortled gleefully. "Sit down, sit down." He waited until Bud was seated. "You come down after the horses?"

"I hope so. Sorry I couldn't give you much to go on. I just heard about the tattoos by accident."

The cheerfulness washed off Rhodes' face. "Good thing you did. I never would have located them without that information."

"How did you check the tattoos?" Bud asked curiously.

"I was just riding along and saw this bunch of strange-looking horses in Broady's pasture. I know most of the

horses Broady keeps around, and I'd never seen these. I
rode into the pasture to check on the brands, and not a
damned one of them was branded. Then what Nix told me
popped into my head. I thought I'd bettter check closer.
You know, I had to rope every one of those horses to be
able to look at that tattoo."

"What if Broady had come along and caught you?"

Rhodes grinned whimsically. "Then I'd have had to do
some tall talking to get out of it, if my badge wasn't
enough."

He reached into a desk drawer and pulled out a piece
of paper. "I jotted down those tattoos and brought them
with me. Do these mean anything to you?"

Bud had brought a list of Kaiser's tattooed horses with
him. He pulled it out of his pocket and compared it with
the list Rhodes had handed him. "You found eight of
them," he announced.

"Good," Rhodes said in triumph. "Broady's operation
has been on the shady side for quite a while. Receiving
stolen horses will put the lid on it."

"Enough to make him squeal?" Bud asked. "I want to
find out who actually stole the horses."

"I think he'll lose all control of his tongue," Rhodes said
with satisfaction. "Ready to go out to his place?"

"As ready as I'll ever be."

On the way to the livery stable, Rhodes asked, "What
do you think of our town? Or have you seen enough of it
to form an opinion?"

"I like it fine except for one thing: the damned wind.
Does it always blow like this?"

"You don't call this little breeze a wind?" Rhodes
scoffed. "I've seen it so bad that it'd blow a man out of his
saddle."

Bud felt the tug of his hat against the chin strap. "This
is enough for me," he grunted.

Rhodes shook his head in mock sorrow. "I'm afraid you'd
never make a good Texan. Too bad, because it's the land
of opportunity. You don't know what you're missing. One
day last year the wind blew so hard it scraped all the
feathers off of Hiram Jones' chickens. Then he got the

idea to see if he could raise naked chickens. He waited until he got a batch of eggs out of them, then hatched them. Do you know those chicks were born without a single feather? Hiram thinks he's got a gold mine. Think of the blessing it will be to housewives not to have to pluck those chickens for a meal."

Bud studied Rhodes. His face was sober enough, but he couldn't disguise the twinkle in his eyes. "Remind me never to get in a poker game with you. You'd always be trying to run a sandy on me."

Rhodes laughed uproariously and whacked Bud on the back. "For a moment, I thought I had you. What gave me away?"

"The gleam in your eyes that called you a liar," Bud replied solemnly.

Rhodes laughed harder. When he caught his breath he said, "You'll do. Do you know I've told that story to drummers who were in Amarillo for the first time. They swallowed it hook, line and sinker. I even promised to take them out and show them those chickens." The twinkle was kindling in his eyes again. "But somehow official business always interfered. I'm even beginning to believe that story myself. Maybe I should ride out there and see those chickens."

Bud was grinning as he mounted. He followed Rhodes out of the stable and touched Lucky lightly with his spurs to catch up.

They turned east, and Rhodes said, "We've got about a fifteen-mile trip. Let me talk to Broady. He's a big hulk with a lot of bluster, and I'll enjoy squashing some of it. I doubt if I can pin anything on him, but he'll be shaking before I'm through."

"You don't know how grateful I am to you," Bud said. "There's a couple of people back in Chandler who doubt me." He was silent a moment. Then there was Lilah. How he wanted her to be proud of him!

"It's nothing," Rhodes said quietly. "It gives me a hold on you." He grinned slyly. "A man's got a right to call in any debts due him, hasn't he?"

"Yes, if *you* don't come collecting," Bud said, and grinned.

Broady lived in a big frame house, sadly in need of repairs. It had been too many years since it had known a coat of paint.

Rhodes looked at the house and shook his head. "It's easy to see that Broady doesn't spend much money on his house. He lives out here with a big, blowsy woman. I've heard talk he picked her up out of a brothel." He shrugged and said whimsically, "That's none of my affair. He's got four or five hundred acres here. He picks up a dollar any way he can. He's not too careful at being legal, but we just haven't been able to nail him. Maybe this time he's slipped. I wonder how far he could have gone if he hadn't had that crooked streak in him." Dusty shook his head. "One of these days, his timing will run short. Maybe this is the day."

Rhodes rode up to the house and threw off. Bud followed suit.

"Broady," Rhodes bawled. "Get out here!"

Broady came to the door, followed by the big blowsy woman. He gave the law officers a sweeping survey, and Bud wondered if he imagined a flicker of unease in those bulging eyes.

"Mel, throw them off," the woman said. "They got no right to pester you."

A flush of rage swept across Broady's face. "Shut your mouth, woman," he hissed. He stepped out of the door and crossed the porch. He came down the steps, a false smile of greeting on his face. "Howdy, Dusty. What can I do for you? You hire a new man?" His eyes touched questioningly on Bud.

"He's not on the force, Mel," Rhodes answered. "He's a lawman out of Oklahoma. He's on the track of some stolen horses."

Bud was sure he saw a touch of fear in Broady's eyes; his mouth had partially opened as though he was sucking in a lungful of air.

"He won't do any good here," Broady said. His voice

was pitched higher than normal, and he couldn't hide the quaver in it.

"We'll see, Mel," Rhodes answered easily. "Let's go look over your horses."

They looked at three different bunches of horses, and each time Rhodes shook his head. "Not the ones I have in mind, Mel."

Broady's assurance was growing. "Then I don't know what you're talking about. You've seen everything I have."

"Not quite," Rhodes purred. "You're holding eight horses in that little pasture at the back of your place. It's pretty well hidden. I just happened to run across it the other day."

Broady's cheeks tightened, and there was stark fear in his eyes. He gulped, licked his lips, and repeated, "I don't know what you're talking about."

Rhodes' eyes and voice had hardened. "Then maybe I can show you. This way."

He led the way to the pasture, surrounded on all sides by a line of hedge trees. The trees were old, for their trunks had thickened. Their long, thorny branches had entangled, making it almost impossible for a man or horse to enter the pasture if they didn't want to be picked apart by those little fishhook thorns. The only entrance to the pasture was at the southwest corner, where somebody had kept a gate cleared of the entangling branches.

"As long as I've been around here," Rhodes said in a conversational tone, "I never knew this pasture was here. I just happened to be passing by, and I caught a glimpse of horses—horses I never saw around here before. I went in and looked more closely at them. Yours, Mel?"

"Just some old plugs I picked up cheap," Broady said disparagingly. "Thought I might make a few dollars out of them. I keep them away from my better horses."

Rhodes cocked his head. "That so? Look like pretty good horses to me. All mares, young enough to be bred. We're not talking about the same horses, Mel."

Broady sounded as though he was having trouble with his breathing, and his face had paled. He kept mopping at his forehead, and the day wasn't that hot.

"Wouldn't I know the value of horses?" he pleaded.

"I sure would've thought so," Rhodes answered mockingly. "Let's go in for a closer look at them." He led the way to the gate and said, "Open it, Mel." His eyes flicked to Bud, and they carried a warning.

Bud kept a close eye on Broady. He thought the man might bolt at any instant, and moved his horse to block any possible attempt.

Broady studied him, then apparently gave up the idea, for he threw off and opened the gate.

"Bring Mel's horse," Rhodes said. He was enjoying this moment, for deviltry danced in his eyes. He must have wanted the man badly, and this was the first chance he saw to get him.

"Close it, Mel," Rhodes called. He waited until Broady closed the gate, then said. "It isn't far—you can walk it."

The eight horses bunched at the approach of the three men, then bolted and ran around the pasture.

"Move pretty good, don't they?" Rhodes said as he watched the horses run. "Look better than old plugs to me. Look like thoroughbreds."

"I know what I bought," Broady said. His lips were dry, and he kept licking them.

"Then you've got the bill of sale."

Broady's face was a ruin. "I had it," he said weakly. "I must've misplaced it. I can't remember where I put it."

"Why don't you quit this damned nonsense?" Rhodes snapped. "You can tell us about it now, or let us find out the hard way."

Broady stared at the ground, pulling at his fingers.

"All right," Rhodes said. "The hard way." There was a new ring in his tone. "Watch him close, Bud. If he tries to get away, shoot him."

Bud drew his pistol. "I think I'd enjoy that," he said.

Rhodes uncoiled his rope as he rode. Bud watched him, admiration showing on his face. Dusty was not only a competent horseman, he knew how to handle a rope.

The horses had retreated to a far corner of the pasture. They scattered wildly in all directions as Rhodes neared them. Even at this distance, Bud could hear their squall of terror.

Dusty had his eyes fixed on one mare, and he kept after her. He made his cast, the loop settled down around the mare's neck, and he dragged her back to where Bud and Broady stood. By the time he reached the two men, the fight was ebbing from her.

"She's meek enough," Bud commented.

Rhodes dropped to the ground. "All of them are. I found that out the other day. Get your list ready."

Using his horse's weight as an anchor, he went hand over hand down the rope until he reached the mare. He fondled her briefly and said, "Good girl. See, everything's all right."

She tossed her head at his first attempt to look into her upper lip, but finally subsided.

"265435," he announced.

"It's on the list," Bud said. "No doubt these are the stolen horses, Dusty."

"What the hell's all this about?" Broady blustered. He was literally shaking.

"You bought stolen horses, Mel," Rhodes said with good humor. "They didn't need branding. They're tattooed on their upper lips. Too bad you didn't know about that."

"I don't believe you," Broady said. His lips quivered, and he looked like a man ready to break into tears.

Rhodes chuckled. "Believe it, Mel." He flipped the restraining loop from the mare's neck; coiling up his rope, he went back to his horse. He swung up and said, "I'll catch another one. Think that'll be enough?"

"Plenty," Bud assured him.

Rhodes caught up another mare and dragged her back to where the two men waited. He inspected the lip and said, "265432."

Bud studied his list. "Check. That's enough, Dusty."

"They're all tattooed," Rhodes said soberly. "I checked every one of them the other day."

Broady was so scared his face was turning a light green. "What's all this mean? I bought those horses legitimately. You trying to point a finger at me?"

"A big finger," Rhodes said calmly. "Buying stolen horses will look as bad to the court as selling them. Hold out your wrists, Mel," He pulled a pair of handcuffs out of his hip pocket.

Broady looked as though he would make a break. "You can't take me in. By God, you haven't got any proof."

"All we need," Rhodes said cheerfully. "Get it out of your mind, Mel. You try to run, and I'll shoot you in the leg. You know I won't miss."

Broady's shoulders sagged. He looked as though he was falling apart. He held out his wrists, and Rhodes snapped the cuffs on them.

"Can't we talk about this?" Broady begged.

"You might do yourself some good," Rhodes said reflectively. "Who sold the horses to you?"

"I swear to God I didn't know them. They made me a good price, and I grabbed it."

"It won't go down, Mel," Rhodes said scornfully. "I know you better than that. You've been too clever."

"How many men drove them here?" Bud snapped.

Broady looked at the ground. "Five. They approached me in the night. I couldn't get a good look at them."

"Let's go, Mel," Rhodes ordered. "We've heard enough."

"Wait a minute," Broady begged. "I swear I didn't know them. I couldn't pass up the chance to buy horses so cheap, could I?"

Rhodes grinned. "You mean those old plugs? I think you've just bought yourself some hard time."

"What did those men look like?" Bud asked. "Surely you got a look at them."

"One of them was a big ox," Broady replied sullenly. "He wore a beard. There was nothing outstanding about the others."

That was no help. The country was full of big, bearded men. "Didn't you hear a name?" Bud asked.

Broady's forehead furrowed. "I did hear one name. A couple of the others called the big man Toby."

Rhodes was watching the play of emotion of Bud's face. "That do you any good?"

"I think it does," Bud said with wicked satisfaction. Every contact he'd had with Toby was bad. Maybe this would be the last one.

Rhodes helped Broady onto his horse. "Better hold on," he advised. "We won't cry if you fall off on your head."

Broady grabbed desperately at the horn with his manacled hands. Rhodes picked up the reins of Broady's horse and led it toward the pasture gate. Bud threw off, opened the gate, and waited for Rhodes and Broady to come through.

Rhodes detected worry in Bud's face. "We'll be back after the horses just as soon as we take him in."

They rode past the house. The woman must have been watching for them, because she came out on the porch. Her eyes widened at the sight of the cuffs on Broady's wrists.

"What's that for?" she asked shrilly.

"Mel's been a bad boy," Rhodes replied cheerfully. "He's been dealing in stolen horses."

"You arresting him?" Her voice had faded to a whisper.

"Looks like it," Rhodes replied.

Tears leaked out of her eyes and streaked down her fat cheeks. "Mel, I told you not to deal with those men. I warned you. What am I going to do all alone here?"

"You shut your mouth," Broady said furiously.

"If you tell the judge what you know, you might pick up a few dollars," Rhodes offered.

Her tears stopped, and she looked at Broady with loathing. "He never gave a damn what happened to me," she said hotly. "I'll tell you everything I know."

Rhodes winked at Bud. That testimony might include prior deals, and it ought to be enough to convict Broady. "Fine," he said softly. "I'll send for you the day he goes on trial."

Chapter 15

Lilah had breathed a sigh of relief when Bud left. The egotistical self-centeredness in men: Once they received a little encouragement, they believed they literally swept a woman off her feet.

She scrubbed the back of her hand across her lips, then spat at the ground. She didn't want Bud's kisses. She remained still for a few more minutes. She had tried to pull out of Bud where the trip was taking him and the reason for it. He had remained silent. Did it in some way involve Toby? That question had plagued her with claws that dug into her mind. But Bud was gone, and by his own words he wouldn't be back for a week or ten days. She'd better use that time to advantage; she had better go see Toby.

She walked into the saloon and called Butch over. He was an excellent floorman, and she could trust him to a point.

"Butch, I'm going to be gone for a while tonight. Look after the place for me."

Butch was a big man, good looking in a coarse way, but he was soft. Indoor work had loosened his muscles and turned him to flab. He had never appealed to Lilah physically. When he first came to work for her, his eyes had been filled with her. The longer he worked for her, the more venturesome he became. She had ignored his first tentative advances, then he became bolder. Surely he could learn from those turndowns, but he hadn't. The last time, she had slashed the edge of her hand into his face, splitting his lips. He stood there in dismay, pressing a handkerchief to his leaking lips.

"You didn't have to do that," he protested.

"Didn't I?" she returned coldly. "I tried every way I know to show you that I wasn't interested. Don't you like working here?" Her voice was icy.

That scared him, for Lilah saw the skin tighten around his eyes and heard the audible suck of his breath. "Sure I do."

"Then act like it," she snapped. "I never encouraged you, yet you still keep trying."

He saw how thoroughly angry she was, and he tried to placate her. "You're a beautiful woman," he said huskily. "You don't realize how hard working around you is without the privilege of touching you."

He meant that as a compliment, but Lilah didn't take it so. "Get it out of your mind," she said, and her lips thinned. "One more time, and you're fired."

Butch looked at the floor. He wouldn't raise his eyes to hers, and she could tell how scared her threat made him. He pulled at his fingers, popping the knuckles. "It won't happen again," he muttered.

"See that it doesn't," she said crisply.

He never made another advance toward her, but she wasn't out of his head. She could see it in the thoughts shining from his eyes. He knew or guessed that she was interested in another man, and she didn't give a damn. The thought of his soft flabbiness pressing against her contrasted with the hard muscular arms of Toby. She couldn't stop the little shudder running through her.

"How long will you be gone, Lilah?"

She shrugged angrily. She didn't know, and if she did, she wasn't telling him. He knew she was going to meet somebody, for there was a nasty little smirk on his face.

Lilah walked out of the door without looking back. She was certain his eyes were fixed on her all the way.

She got her riding mare out of the livery stable, barely nodding to Little's greeting. This was the way she wanted it, this cold withdrawal. It let her stay aloof from all people.

She sniffed at Little's offer to help her up. She had gotten along this far without accepting all the courtesies that men insisted upon proffering and women considered a necessity. She didn't look back as she rode out of the stable. She knew that Little was watching her and probably shaking his head in disapproval. She didn't give a damn what Little or anybody else thought.

She rode down the street at a brisk canter. She didn't see the boy come out of the shadows, stare at her a moment, then break into a brisk run, trying to keep up with her.

Billy waited at the same corner where he had seen Lilah the night before. He didn't really dislike her, but she was a woman, and Billy dismissed the entire category.

He had his mount tethered to a tree a few paces away. Charley wasn't fast, but he was enduring. He could keep up that plodding pace as long as Billy requested it. Billy loved him; besides, he was the best Elmer could afford.

He stiffened as he heard the brisk trotting of a horse coming this way. He didn't see the horse or rider for a moment, then they came into view.

Billy sucked in a triumphant breath. It was Lilah again, and she was riding the same route. He knew there was no hope of keeping up with her, but he could keep close enough to eliminate the possibility of completely losing her.

Lilah didn't see him, and he doubted she would have paid any atttention to him if she had. Something was on her mind, and whatever it was, she was completely engrossed in it.

Billy waited until she was at the far end of the block before he untied Charley. He sprang up onto his back and said, "Let's go, boy."

Charley sighed lugubriously and cast Billy a reproachful glance. He didn't believe in any unnecessary effort, preferring to doze in the shade of a tree.

Billy's heels drummed against Charley's flanks. Each

time he rode, he had to go through this routine to convince Charley that he meant business.

Lilah was out of sight now, but Billy knew the direction she had taken. There wasn't much out that way. He kept drumming on Charley, and finally got him going in an awkward, shambling lope. Billy knew he wasn't going to cover much ground at this rate, but he had to keep going.

His brow was furrowed as he tried to recall what lay out in this direction. The soil tailed off quickly, picking up too much sand, and Billy couldn't think of a single productive farm out here. Then his face brightened. The old Grimes' place was out here—but it had been abandoned for several years now. After his wife's death, Grimes had become a recluse. After Grimes' death, nobody seemed to want his place. The town used to talk unfeelingly about Grimes' predicament: He didn't want help from anybody, and he rarely came into town.

Out of curiosity a couple of years ago, Billy had ridden Charley out this way. The house was a wreck. The roof was sagging, and most of the windows were broken out. A shiver ran through him. It had an air about it that he couldn't describe. Maybe Grimes' ghost was still hanging about the place. Spooky was the right word to describe it.

Billy was certain Lilah was heading out to that ruin of a house, and he wondered why. There couldn't be a thing out there that she could possibly want.

The moon came out of the scudding clouds just as Charley topped a steep hill. The light made Billy feel better, and he could see. Far ahead he could pick out the diminishing figure of Lilah and her horse. There was no possible way of catching up, and all Billy wanted to learn was where she was going. He'd also like to know why, but that would have to wait until he got there.

The house looked worse than last time as he approached it, and the moonlight cruelly picked out its advancing state of deterioration. He knew a stab of disappointment with the first glance: Lilah's horse wasn't there. Billy started to turn Charley away when a thought struck him. Lilah could have left her horse around back, hidden from the sight of the road.

The idea was worth exploring, but he didn't want to ride right up to the house. He slithered from Charley's back and started out cautiously on foot, moving in a wide, cautious circle. There was nothing to catch or hold his attention until he came to the rear. He had guessed right. There was Lilah's horse.

He hunkered down, keeping his eyes fixed on one of the windows in the rear. Something was different about that window, and it took a moment of hard thinking to decide what it was. Then he had it: All the windows he had passed in making his way around the house had been gaping, as though some mischievous kids had grabbed the opportunity to heave rocks through them. This one was blank, but it was curtained with some kind of material to cut off the light behind it.

Billy's senses quickened, and he didn't care how long it took to find out whether his guesses were accurate.

"Watch your step," Toby advised. "This old house is falling apart. The floor is littered with boards."

"Didn't you think of cleaning it up?" Lilah asked. "You've been out here long enough." She couldn't see his expression, but she knew he was unimpressed. Another of Toby's faults was that he was lazy.

She picked her steps carefully, and twice her shoe brushed a piece of board. The interior was dark and musty. Toby struck a match, and she asked sharply, "What are you doing?"

"Why, I'm going to light a lamp," he said in mild surprise.

"With that window uncovered?" she demanded angrily.

"It wouldn't make any difference," he said carelessly. "Nobody comes out here anymore."

"Cover that window first, Toby." At his hesitation, her face turned ugly. "I mean it." They were always at each other over some small matter like this.

He saw the familiar hardening in her face and said meekly. "All right, Lilah, if that's what you want. I sent Gabe into town several days ago to buy a few supplies. I told him to include blankets, nails, and a hammer. I thought of making a few repairs, but when I saw how much there was to do, I gave up."

Lilah's displeasure didn't lessen. Toby had no drive in him. If he had, he would try to make this place a little more livable.

She held a blanket up to the window while Toby hammered in a few nails to hold it in place. "Does this suit your majesty?" he asked mockingly.

"Oh, stop it," she said crossly. "You can light that lamp now." She'd never understand how Toby could be content to spend so much of his time in darkness. Then a thought startled her: Maybe he hadn't. Maybe he had used the lamp despite the danger to him and the others.

The strenghtening flame drove the shadows into the corners, and for the first time Lilah saw the other two men hunkered down in a corner. It gave her an eerie feeling to think of those eyes being on her without her being aware of it.

She nodded to them. "Cass, Gabe," she murmured.

Neither of them said anything, but their teeth flashed in dark faces. Something was wrong. She had sent four men out here to live with Toby until things settled down, and she learned what the new marshal was going to do.

"Where's Verl and Slate?" she demanded.

"Sent them out on a little job," Toby said easily.

Lilah's senses sharpened. Was Toby trying to be evasive? She hadn't okayed any job, and he had gone ahead without waiting to talk to her.

"What job?"

Toby squirmed under her probing eyes. "I saw a chance to pick up a few easy dollars," she said, not looking at her. "On the way out here, we seen two good-looking two-year-olds in Pardee Quincy's pasture. I decided to pick them up. Hell, it was simple. Pardee doesn't keep any help. I sent Verl and Slate back to get them."

"Where are those two-year-olds now, Toby?"

The deceptive softness of her voice didn't stop his squirming. "I sent them on to Colorado. Verl and Slate should be back this week. Damn it, Lilah," he said petulantly. "I did it only because of you."

Her eyes flamed. Now he was laying the blame solely on her. "How do you figure that?"

He glanced unhappily at Cass and Gabe, and Lilah guessed at Toby's thoughts. He didn't like being questioned before those two.

"Cass, Gabe," she directed. "I brought some supplies out with me. They're behind my saddle. Go out and get them."

She sensed the disappointment in them as they slowly got to their feet and shuffled out of the house. Now she could have it out with Toby.

"Damn it, Toby," she said passionately, "why do you think I sent you and the others out here?"

His anger was rising, making his cheekbones look sharper. "Certainly not for our comfort," he sneered.

"You poor fool," she said contemptuously. "I wanted you out of town until I learned more about that new marshal. Get that look off your face. He's already proven he can handle himself. You should know that."

Toby hung his head, and Lilah imagined it was to hide the shame in his face. "He was lucky with me. I want another chance at him."

"Keep on the way you're going," she said heatedly, "and you're liable to get it." She was silent a moment. "He proposed to me."

That startled Toby, for he raised his head and stared at her. "You clawed his face?" Toby cried.

Lilah shook her head. "I told him I'd consider it while he was gone."

"He's gone?"

"For a week or ten days," she murmured.

"Where's he gone and why?"

She shook her head. "I couldn't get it out of him. Damn it, can't you see that if I can tie his hands, I'll make him helpless?"

Toby's hands were bunched, and he was furious. "You can't marry him. You're married to me."

"But he doesn't know that," she said. "If I can keep him thinking I might, can't you see what it'll do?"

He walked over to her and gripped her shoulders. She

felt the bite of his powerful fingers. "What about us? I thought I meant something to you. Do you think I want you playing around with another man?"

Lilah shrugged off his hands. "You still do mean everything to me. But I grew up poor. I lived too long like that. I swore I'd change things. I would have, too, if that damned marshal hadn't happened along."

Toby had never sought to learn how much money they had made on their horse raids. Money was the least important thing in his life. He was content to do as she directed as long as he knew she belonged to him. She had a clever mind. Her saloon gave her the advantage of knowing what was going on in the town and surrounding country. That was how she had learned about Kaiser and his mares. She could gather information and sort it out to her advantage. She picked out all the targets, as well as the markets where they could sell their spoils. Oh, he had changed her orders when he took the Kaiser mares to Texas, but she couldn't complain on that point. It had been a good sale, bringing more money than she expected. But the thought that she might be considering another man's arms frightened him. She could be thinking of cutting him loose.

"You've made a lot of money, Lilah," he pleaded. "Why don't we just take it and go. You should be sick of this country by now. If this marshal is as smart as you think he is, it could be getting dangerous. We could light out for California."

Lilah stubbornly shook her head. "I set an amount of money in my mind. I haven't quite reached it. A few more successful raids, and I'll be there."

She was pleased by the unhappy silence that seized him. This talk should scare him. From now on, he wouldn't get any more wild ideas of his own.

"I came out to tell you that Owen Parnell has finally bought that stallion he's been bragging about for so long. God, how many nights I've listened to his drunken boasting about that animal. It's the finest walking horse that ever came out of Tennessee, and he's finally bought it. He'll be delivered in a day or two, and if Parnell paid as much money for it as he bragged, it'll be one of our biggest steals. With that marshal gone for a week or so, there'll be no better time to pick up that stallion." Her eyes challenged him. "Are you man enough to go get it?"

His eyes fired with a new hope. That was only talk about her interest in another man. She still needed him.

"Parnell's a tough customer," he said musingly. "He'll keep a close eye on that stallion, at least for a while."

"You're not clever enough to get it?" she taunted.

"I didn't say that," he corrected. "Let me think about it."

Cass and Gabe came back into the room, carrying two gunny bags. The bags clinked as they walked.

"Lilah told me something interesting," Toby drawled. "Owen Parnell bought an expensive stallion. Lilah thinks we should pick it up."

Cass looked worried. "I know that Parnell. He's one hardnosed character. We'd better wait until Slate and Verl get back."

Toby made an impatient motion. "We don't need them. How many men do you think it takes to do a simple job?"

Gabe was unloading the gunny bags on the rickety table. "Maybe the surroundings aren't elegant, but the food sure is. Lilah, you thought of everything."

Lilah smiled at him. The brief rebellion in her help was settled. She moved toward the door. "I won't be back unless something comes up. You stay under cover until you hear from me."

She had no concern about the money Parnell's stallion would bring. As long as she kept Toby and the others amply supplied with the material things, actual money never bothered them.

Toby walked out with Lilah. He looked back at the house, then swept her into his arms. He hugged her so tightly that her breath exploded from her lungs. All her resentment at some of the stupid things he did vanished.

"You had me scared back there for a moment," he murmured. "I thought you were thinking of leaving me."

"Not as long as you stay in line," she replied and lifted her face to his seeking lips.

Billy saw two men come out and take sacks from the back of a horse, then go back inside. He stiffened a few minutes later as a man and a woman came out of the back door. They stepped into a patch of moonlight, and Billy could see them plainly. The man was big with a thick beard.

His eyes grew big in wonder as he watched them embrace. Lilah seemed starved for the big man's kisses. Billy breathed harder, and his heart was going at a furious rate. Did he have something to tell Bud when he returned! Hearing this might be a terrible blow, but he had to be told.

Billy realized he had better get out of there while those two were absorbed in each other. He slithered away, knowing instinctively that this was a poor time for either of them to discover him.

He didn't straighten up until he reached Charley. He untied the donkey and led him farther away from the road, stopping in a fairly thick grove of trees. This should hide him from Lilah's eyes.

Billy waited a good ten minutes before he heard the thud of horse hooves. Lilah wasn't riding terribly fast, but Billy knew he could never keep up with her, even if he wanted to. He only wanted to get back to town without her being aware that he had followed her.

He was sweating when he finally released Charley's muzzle. "Good boy," he muttered. "We can go home now."

Chapter 16

Cass made a trip into town. It was almost midnight when he rode back to the old house. His excitement showed in the way he threw off and rushed inside.

Toby looked up indifferently from the game of solitaire he was playing. The cards were old and battered, and four of them were missing. Each time he came to a spot where one of the missing cards would have fit, he credited himself with a win.

"Cass, you look like somebody is hot on your tail. It's not that, is it?"

Cass literally stuttered in his excitement. "Parnell came into Lilah's saloon tonight. All he could talk about was the new stallion that was delivered to his place today. He bragged about what it cost him so much that somebody said, 'With a horse that valuable, it seems to me you'd be scared to death of somebody stealing him."

"Then Parnell said, 'I keep eight men out there, and every one of them is a crack shot. Let somebody even try to get near that horse, and he'll get his damned head blown off.' "

Toby chuckled complacently. "Owen always did have a big mouth."

"You think he doesn't mean that?" Cass asked indignantly. "He's got enough money he can do anything he wants. He can afford to pay his help top wages, and they'll do what Parnell orders them for fear of losing that good-paying job. I'm telling you nobody is going to get near that horse."

Toby's chuckle didn't stop. "We are. Did you get that kerosene I ordered?"

"Five gallons of it," Cass said unhappily. "Do you know how hard it is to carry a five-gallon tin on horseback?"

"You got it back here, didn't you?" Toby asked, undisturbed by Cass's indignation. "I think tonight would be a good time to go after that stallion."

"Jesus Christ," Cass said, appalled. "So soon after that stallion's been delivered? Those guards will really be on their toes."

"Maybe," Toby said, unperturbed. "Is Parnell keeping him in that big barn back of the house?"

"That's part of what Parnell was boasting about," Cass said bleakly. "He's had that big barn redone. He claims it's better living quarters than most men have." He looked sullenly about their wreck of a house. "It wouldn't have to be much better to beat us."

Toby slapped his thigh and laughed. "You're sure crying your heart out tonight."

Cass stubbornly shook his head. "I just don't like those armed guards waiting for us. You're not even giving them a little time to settle down."

Toby walked to the door, stepped outside, and cocked an eye at the sky. "A perfect night for it," he mused. "The moon will be late rising. Let's go."

"I just got back from a trip to town," Cass said wrathfully. "Don't you think I ever get tired?"

"Remind me tomorrow to feel sorry for you," Toby said unfeelingly. "You can take a long rest then." He inspected the lashing on the tin of kerosene. It was secure. "As long as it's riding so well, I don't see any need of changing horses."

Cass's mouth opened to howl, then slowly closed as Toby stared at him. He had already done a lot of complaining. Toby could only be pushed so far. He climbed on his burdened horse with no further comment.

The three rode without exchanging a word. Toby could

feel their resentment pounding at him. Their disapproval of this risky trip was obvious in their silence. Well, the completion of a successful job would change that.

Parnell's money was evident in his place. The fences were all up and painted. The house and outbuildings were set a good mile back from the road.

Toby halted the other two at the entrance. "We'd better walk in. Some nervous finger could see us riding in and blow us out of the saddle." He caught the shiver running through Gabe and asked mockingly, "The thought of that scare you, Gabe?"

"You're damned right it does," Gabe said heatedly. "We've never been up against something like this before. We're playing against a stacked deck."

"Maybe not," Toby said reflectively. "I've got a joker that Parnell doesn't even know about." He slid down and led his horse well off the road, then secured it in a little copse of trees. He helped Cass untie the tin of kerosene and grunted as he lowered it to an arm's length. "We'll know we're carrying it before we get to the house."

He looked back after a few paces. "Good," he said. "If anybody does pass this way, they'll never see those horses."

Halfway to the house, the three left the lane, climbing the fence to cut through the pasture behind it. It was tougher walking, for the grass was lush. It kept tangling around their boots, pulling at them.

"Damned hard walking," Cass grumbled as he almost went down.

"Keep your voice down," Toby hissed. "We're not too far from the house."

"Think anybody's up at this hour to hear me?" Cass jeered, but he lowered his voice.

They stopped a hundred yards from the house. Even on a moonless night, it was white and ghostly.

Toby stared at it for a long moment. "See any signs of life?" he whispered.

The other two shook their heads. "If Parnell does have those guards he bragged about, they'll be at the barn," Cass whispered back.

Toby looked at the big barn. It loomed above the house, and there must be bettter than two hundred yards between the two buildings. "You two go around the house and close in on the barn," he ordered. "Just be sure you're not seen."

"What are you going to do?" Cass asked.

"I'll join you just as soon as I get a little job done. It won't take long. Then you'll see how I plan to take that stallion."

They moved away slowly. The dark night was a Godsend. Those two figures would be difficult to see.

Toby waited until they were out of sight, then approached the house. His greatest danger was in the last thirty yards. The windows looked like blank eyes, and there was no way of telling who stood behind them. Toby's skin tensed in anticipation of a bullet. If someone saw him, they would shoot before they asked questions.

Toby crawled the last few yards, dragging the tin behind him. He was sweating profusely and cringing inwardly when he reached the house. This was the dangerous part. If he didn't have a few undisturbed moments, somebody could drop him in his tracks.

He uncapped the tin and splashed a generous portion of the liquid onto the wood. The pungent odor of the kerosene rose and bit at his nostrils. It could reach somebody in the house and arouse them to make an inspection. There was always that possibility, but Toby discarded the slight chance. At this hour, anybody in the house should be asleep, and the odor wouldn't awaken them.

He went around the house in a crouch, splashing kerosene every step or two. It kept tickling his nostrils, making him want to cough. How many sleeping people were in the house? Toby's conscious mind didn't even entertain the question. Getting out of the burning house was their problem.

He had almost made a circle of the house when he ran out of kerosene. It didn't matter. What gaps there were in the kerosene-splashed boards would be quickly filled in by the leaping fire. His fingers were shaking so that he failed in striking the first two matches. He muttered a curse at the wind that whipped out the weak flames. Once he got the fire started, the wind would be to his advantage, driving the fire before it.

He carefully shielded his third match and moved his cupped hand until he almost touched the kerosene-soaked board. Hah, he thought exultantly as the feeble flame sprang into furious life when he touched it to the moistened board. He set three more fires, and in just these few moments the wind-driven fire was sweeping flames the length of the house.

Toby would have liked to set fires in more places, but he knew he'd better get out of here. At any moment, somebody would discover the fire and scream an alarm. So he worked his way toward the barn, looking back a couple of times. The flame had engulfed the rear wall of the house, and Toby was surprised that it hadn't been discovered yet.

He was getting closer to the barn than he wanted, and he looked impatiently for Cass and Gabe. Where in the hell were they? He didn't dare call out to them.

"Over here, Toby," he heard a reedy whisper. He crawled that way, and Cass and Gabe were right before him.

"My God, you set fire to the house," Cass said in an awed whisper.

Toby snorted. The dummy should have figured that out for himself. What did he think the kerosene was for? "Can you think of a better way to pull those guards to the house?" he hissed.

"What if there's people in the house?" Cass couldn't hide the tremor in his voice.

"That's their problem," Toby said, with brutal candor. "Finding a way to get at that stallion is mine. Have you seen any of the guards?"

Gabe nodded. "A few seconds ago, two of them came to the door and looked out. They went back in. We haven't seen any more of them."

Toby looked at the burning house. The red in the sky tinted his face. "Somebody's going to discover it any minute now," he muttered.

Gabe looked at Toby. "One of the guards is looking out the barn door," he whispered.

Three pairs of eyes swiveled to the figure silhouetted against the dark, oblong shape of the door. They couldn't make out his expression, but his terror-filled cry told them what he was feeling.

"Good God!" the guard screamed. "The house is on fire! All of you get out here! On the run!"

The guards poured out of the barn door, and the thud of their feet carried faintly to the three watching men.

Toby counted them as they passed. "All eight of them," he said, triumph in his voice. "The fire will keep them occupied for some time. Let's go."

Cass held back. "What if there's another guard or two left in there? We could be walking right into some hot lead."

Toby looked at him with disgust. "You were the one who reported hearing Parnell's word He said he hired eight guards. Eight guards just passed us. That cleaned all of them out. You gonna waste more time arguing about it?"

"I guess not," Cass muttered."

They made a slinking run toward the barn and slipped through the door. Toby paused to catch his breath. He glanced around the barn, and there was no sign of another guard. "All clear," he said.

Cass and Gabe were just inside the door, looking toward the house. The fire's radiance illuminated the land around it as plainly as daylight.

"I just saw Parnell and his wife run out of the house," Cass announced. "They got out."

"That make you feel better?" Toby sneered.

"It does," Cass said stubbornly. "I wouldn't want to see anybody burn to death."

"Maybe that'll get you into Heaven," Toby jeered. "Can we get to work now?"

They went down the left hand side of the double line of stalls, stopping momentarily to peer into each one. They were coming back up the other side when Toby announced, "Here he is."

The light wasn't too good, but all three got the impression of a magnificent animal, his size making the stall look cramped.

The stallion snorted nervously and threw up its head.

"Easy now, boy," Toby said in a soothing voice. "Nobody's going to harm you."

He picked up a bridle from a rack near the stall, opened the stall door, and slipped inside.

"You be careful," Gabe warned. "You're a stranger to him."

Toby waved Gabe quiet. He knew what he was doing. He was an expert horseman, and horses sensed that quality in him.

The stallion reared, and its fore hooves slammed down against the earthen floor. Toby kept up a quiet crooning. After two more rearings the stallion quieted and stood still, but it still blew nervously at Toby's approach.

Toby reached out and touched him. The stallion jerked its head aside and bared its teeth. Toby reached again, and this time his fingers touched the velvety muzzle. There was something in that touch, for the horse calmed instantly. Toby kept stroking that long, intelligent nose, and he could sense ease flowing through the animal.

"Goodboy," he murmured as he slipped on the bridle.

"You've been in there a long time," Gabe said.

"Shut up," Toby whispered. He knew what he was doing. He didn't want an alien note disturbing the animal. "I'm coming out now," he said, and led the horse out of the stall. "Get me a blanket and saddle."

Cass brought some gear out of the tack room. Toby spread and smoothed out the blanket on the stallion's back. A thought momentarily disturbed him. What if this stallion wasn't broken? No, he thought violently. This horse's actions said it had been broken quite a while back. He set the saddle lightly on the blanket.

The horse flinched, and Toby thought, Oh—oh, here it comes. He was tensed to react to whatever might happen.

The horse steadied. A saddle was no new thing to it.

"Look at that," Cass marveled. "He's got a touch with horses."

Toby grinned and cinched the saddle, testing it for give. This was a big-barreled horse, and Toby couldn't take up any holes in the strap.

"I think I better take him," Toby said. He put a foot in the stirrup and placed most of his weight on the saddle.

"Where are you taking him to?" Gabe asked.

"Out to Jabez Keen's in Colorado. A horse like this should bring a hell of a price. Tell Lilah I'll be back just as soon as I can." The blood ran hot in his veins. He had stolen this horse for her. She should reward him richly, and he wasn't thinking of monetary payment.

"I'll go out the back door," he said. He swung up and sat tentatively a moment. This horse wasn't going to cause him any trouble at all.

"Get out of here as quick as you can," he instructed the two. "Pick up those three horses and take them away. Make a wide swing of the house. Don't let anyone see you."

Cass snorted. "Do you think we're fools? As mad as Parnell will be, I wouldn't let him catch a glimpse of us."

He trotted down the bare aisle and swung the big door on its hangers. Toby loped easily by him, and Cass raised a hand in farewell. That Toby was a genius. He picked up a prize stallion from right under Parnell's nose. The town would be talking about this for weeks to come.

Chapter 17

Rhodes had found a man to go along with Bud to take the horses back to Oklahoma. Bud had settled on a price with him to make the trip, and everybody was satisfied.

"Think you'll have any trouble with them?" Rhodes asked.

"Shouldn't," Bud replied. The eight horses were roped together in a long line. It would cut down their speed, but it also eliminated the possibility of them stampeding.

"Can't tell you how grateful I am, Dusty," Bud said, proffering his hand. "This will put a little respect for the law in a few people's heads."

"Gratitude is on my side," Rhodes said, shaking Bud's hand hard. "Broady's been in my hair for quite a while. He wasn't one of the big criminals, but he was sneaky enough to be an annoyance."

"Think this will put him out of circulation, Dusty?"

"Should," Rhodes said with immense satisfaction. "With the woman against him—" He shook his head and didn't finish. "Let this be a lesson to you. Never cross a woman."

Bud grinned. "Were you going to give me the old saw of hell hath no fury like a woman scorned?"

"Something like that," Rhodes said seriously.

"Think you'll need me at the trial?" Bud asked. "I can get back down here."

"Don't think it'll be necessary. Trial should be in about

a month. If I run into trouble, I'll let you know. And I'll keep an eye out for the remaining horses. Doubt if I'll run across them, but I might."

"I'd appreciate that," Bud said solemnly. He shook hands again and walked outside where the horses and his helper waited.

Sull Thomas was a likable man, a couple of years younger than Bud. He had an engaging grin and a ready laugh.

"All ready, Sull?"

"As ready as I'll ever be."

"This trip won't take too long," Bud assured him.

Thomas flashed an appealing smile. "I was glad to get this job. I'm at loose ends right now."

Bud looked back after a half block. Rhodes still stood in front of his office. He raised a hand, and Bud returned the farewell. There was one hell of a good man. Bud was damned lucky this had worked out so well. He had found the proverbial needle in a pretty big haystack. Well, part of it, he amended. The rest of that needle might have been scattered so thoroughly that he would never run across it. He thought of the irascible old man and grinned. Kaiser might squawk because all of his horses weren't returned. With that waspish nature, he might not stop to consider how fortunate he was to have any of his horses returned.

Thomas looked back at the horses. "Good-looking bunch."

"All thoroughbreds," Bud returned. "We'd never have found them if it hadn't been for the tattoos on their lips."

Thomas looked big-eyed, and Bud said solemnly. "God's truth. All thoroughbreds are identified by the tattoos on the inside of their upper lip."

"I didn't know that."

"Broady didn't, either," Bud said, and chuckled.

Thomas leaned over and patted the neck of his paint pony. "She's not worth anywhere near as much as these thoroughbreds, but I'd sure hate to lose her."

"Everybody's had a few horses he feels like that about," Bud said thoughtfully. "I'd hate to lose this old hammerhead." He patted Lucky.

"I'll bet the owner will be damned glad to get these horses back."

Knowing Kaiser, Bud doubted that. "I hope so," he said soberly.

It took five days to make the trip back to Oklahoma. Bud pointed out the Kaiser house ahead. "That's the place we're looking for."

"I've enjoyed the trip," Thomas said. "Learned something on it. I can't say that for a lot of my trips."

Bud grinned and nodded. They had gotten along well. Thomas was a good man to ride the road with. He was a willing worker, and there never was a complaint out of him.

Clyde was standing out in front of the house when Bud and Thomas came up with the horses. "Holy gee," he said, his eyes as big as dollars. "You brought back some of Mr. Kaiser's horses. He won't believe it."

"I know," Bud said with grim humor. "He said I'd never find any of them. It pleasures me to prove him wrong. Sorry it's not the entire bunch."

"Do you think you'll find the rest of them?"

Bud doubted it, though he said, "I guess time will tell. Will you get Mr. Kaiser out here?"

Clyde had good lungs. His yell would have raised the soundest sleeper. He waited a few seconds, then yelled again. "Mr. Kaiser! Get out here! You've got a surprise!"

Kaiser came to the door, and he looked grumpy. His attention was focused on the man who yelled at him. "Damn it, Clyde, you woke me up from my nap. How many times do I have to tell you nobody wakes me up?"

Clyde's grin was unabashed. "Look over there, Mr. Kaiser. You got a visitor."

Kaiser's eyes swung to Bud. They widened in shock, then traveled on to the horses behind him. "God Almighty," he said in reverent tones. "You got my horses back."

"Not all of them, Mr. Kaiser. Just eight of them."

Kaiser stared in disbelief, then his face darkened. "I lost twenty head."

Bud sighed. The old man was back in form. "I don't

know where the rest of them are," he said unhappily. "You're damned lucky to have this many back."

Kaiser realized he'd gone too far. "I appreciate what you did. Did you shoot the miserable horse thief?"

"He's coming up for trial," Bud said curtly. He had a belly full of this man. "He was the buyer. He wasn't the only one involved in the theft."

"I hope they hang him," Kaiser said viciously. "I got to say one thing, Marshal. You did a hell of a job. I want to show you how much I appreciate it. I'm going to give you a bonus."

Bud didn't know whether or not his office would allow such a gratuity. "Give that bonus to Sull," he directed Kaiser. "Without him, I couldn't have gotten the horses up here." He jerked his head toward Thomas.

"I'll do just that," Kaiser said. "Wait until I go in the house and get some money."

He disappeared inside, and Clyde said in an awed voice. "You musta got to him. Never saw him being reckless with money."

Kaiser came back out, and he handed Thomas fifty dollars. Thomas started to protest, and Kaiser waved him quiet. "It's worth that to me."

Bud felt himself softening to the old man. At least he had put a little respect in him. "Glad to have been of service to you, Mr. Kaiser."

Kaiser made a disparaging motion. "Think there's any chance of getting the rest of them back?" he asked gruffly.

"I don't know," Bud replied honestly. "I've got a lead on the men who did the actual stealing. Maybe if I can stop them, you won't have to worry about losing any more."

"That'd be a relief," Kaiser said as he shook hands with Bud. "It'll let an honest man sleep. You drop by any time you're out here. You hear me, Marshal?"

"I'll do just that," Bud said gravely.

As they rode away, Thomas said, "I saw a rough, old man change right before my eyes. Was he always tough?"

"Always, Sull. He's changed all right. He had no use for

a man wearing a badge. I guess he had every right to feel that way. They didn't do much for him."

Thomas grinned. "He's on your side now."

"And I'm grateful," Bud said soberly. "I'd rather have that old dog wagging his tail at me than baring his fangs. We'll stop in town and get your money." How Crump would howl when Bud presented him a bill for Thomas' help.

Thomas thought a moment, then said hesitantly, "I don't need it. Kaiser gave me more than enough to make up the amount you promised me."

"You rich enough to pass up money that's owing you?"

Thomas thought a moment. "I guess not," he said slowly.

They were silent the remainder of the way into town. They passed the marshal's office, and Billy was sitting before it. He jumped to his feet at the sight of Bud and started to rush out into the street.

Bud waved him back. He appreciated the kid being glad to see him, but he didn't have the time right now to talk to him.

"I'll be right back, Billy," he called.

"But I've got something important to tell you," Billy yelled.

At Billy's age, everything that happened was important. Bud kicked his horse into a faster pace. He didn't want to disappoint the kid, but he couldn't see how holding his information a few minutes could make any difference. Right now, he had to take care of Thomas. He looked back and saw the disappointment spread over Billy's face.

Thomas had caught it all, for he commented, "You didn't leave the kid too happy."

"Maybe not," Bud admitted. "He's kinda appointed himself as a party of one to look after me. At his age, what a kid's doing right now is the most important thing in the world."

"He seems to have a lot of respect for you, Bud. You wouldn't want to destroy that."

"Not for the world," Bud conceded. "I appreciate his

loyalty. I'm just asking him to hold it up for a few minutes."

"I'd get back as soon as I could," Thomas murmured.

Bud was getting weary of this subject. "I intend to." He hoped he didn't have to look all over town for Crump.

But the mayor was just coming out of his house, and there was censure in his eyes at the sight of Bud.

"Did you enjoy your holiday?" Crump asked sarcastically. "I didn't think you were ever coming back."

Bud almost had to bite his tongue to keep from exploding. "It was no holiday, Mayor," he said quietly. "Me and Mr. Thomas"—he jerked his head toward Sull—"just drove eight of Kaiser's thoroughbreds back from Amarillo."

Crump's jaw sagged. "That the truth?" he asked weakly.

"God's truth," Thomas said solemnly.

"That should've pleased the old man," Crump said. "He's raised enough hell about those horses being gone." His manner toward Bud had changed. "How did you happen to get on their trail?"

Bud had no intention of telling him all the details, not until this case was completely wrapped up. "Kaiser lost twenty horses," he reminded Crump. "We brought back only eight."

"Eight is something," Crump exclaimed. "I bet he raised pure hell that you didn't bring back all of them."

Bud's eyes narrowed. "He tried. I pointed out that he was lucky to get back eight of them. That calmed him down." He paused a moment, then said, "I think I know how to break up this rustling ring."

"You better break it up," Crump said harshly. "Two head were stolen from Quincy while you were gone. Parnell lost a prized stallion, and his house burned down."

Bud's face hardened. "You blaming me for that?"

"You weren't here, were you? Nobody was here to cover your office."

At that, Bud wanted to set him back hard. "Mayor, you or the town owes Mr. Thomas forty dollars."

Crump flinched as though Bud had struck him. "What

for?" he bleated. "I never hired him to do anything for me. The town didn't either."

Bud's lips thinned. He expected this argument from Crump. "But I needed help to drive the horses back here. You don't expect *me* to pay for that, do you?"

Crump's nostrils were pinched from the rapidity of his breathing. "How long did he help? Forty dollars is a hell of a price."

"He did his job," Bud said crisply. "We were on the trail five days."

"My God," Crump said in horror. "Forty dollars for five days. Why, that's eight dollars a day. Are you two in cahoots in this?"

Bud's face darkened. "I'll pay the damned forty dollars," he snapped, "but you better start getting yourself a new badge toter. I'm leaving."

"You can't do that," Crump squalled.

"I don't see anything to stop me," Bud said levelly.

"But you said you thought you could smash this horse stealing ring. You can't leave until you do that. You owe this town that—"

Bud's temper exploded the last of his restraint. "I don't owe this town a damned thing." He started toward his horse. "Come with me, Sully."

They hadn't taken four steps before Crump dashed after them. "I'll pay, I'll pay," he panted. "But you're ruining this town."

"Remind me to cry over that tomorrow," Bud said brusquely. He watched Crump grudgingly count forty dollars into Thomas' hand. He had never seen a man suffer so much over the payment of money.

"You're not leaving now," Crump begged after he finished the odious chore.

Bud gave him a frosty grin. "You just removed my reason." He turned back to Thomas, and they remounted. After a few steps, Thomas asked curiously, "Would you have quit your job?"

Bud chuckled. "I hadn't fully decided. But I knew that threat was the best way to move that old miser."

Thomas laughed. "It hasn't been a pleasant place to work has it?"

"I've known better," Bud growled. "But I came here to do a job. It still needs finishing." He prodded Lucky into faster motion. "I've got to get back and see if Billy is still there." That argument with Crump had lasted longer than he had expected. Billy might have given up on him and wandered off.

"He'll be there," Thomas said quietly.

"How do you know that?"

"I saw the way he looked at you. He really believes in you."

"I hope you're right."

Thomas stopped his horse and stretched out a hand. "Never had a more pleasant trip. If another one comes up and you need a hand, let me know."

Bud returned the handshake. It had been a short trip, but he had grown to know Sull. The man was reliable with a keen sense of responsibility. Bud hoped he would always be fortunate enough to hire men of this caliber.

"A good trip back," he said.

"And I hope you catch the ones you want," Thomas returned. He lifted a hand in farewell, then stirred his horse into a lope that would eat up the miles.

Bud watched him for a moment, then moved on toward his office. He hoped Billy was still there and that Billy would forgive him for making him wait.

Chapter 18

Billy's face was set in stubborn lines as he stared straight ahead.

He's really angry with me, Bud thought. "I thought you had something important to tell me, kid."

"It musta not been very important," Billy said in a cutting tone. "You didn't have time to listen."

Bud sighed, and laid a hand on Billy's knee. "Aw, Billy, I'm sorry. I had something that had to be done. I got back just as soon as I could."

"A complete stranger," Billy said disgustedly. "You had more time for him than you had for me."

"He helped me a lot, Billy," Bud said softly. "He helped me bring back some of the horses that were stolen from Mr. Kaiser. He helped change the old man's mind. It made things easier for me. Don't you see?" he finished.

Billy glanced at him out of the corner of his eye. "That the truth?"

"God's truth, Billy. That help may enable me to break up the gang that's been doing all the stealing. I think I know who's behind it."

Billy shook his head. "I'll bet this is more important— how much does Lilah mean to you?"

Bud blinked. That was a blunt and direct question. How could he make Billy understand just how much Lilah meant to him? "She means a lot," he said quietly.

149

Billy stared out into the street and was quiet for so long that Bud was concerned.

"Why don't you just say it, Billy?" he suggested.

Billy made several false starts, then blurted out, "I tried to fellow her the first night you were gone, but I was on foot, and I couldn't keep up with her."

Bud's face turned stiff. "Why would you want to follow her?" There was an edge to his voice.

"I wanted to see that nothing happened to her. I was doing it for you."

The stiffness eased out of Bud's face. He reached over and gripped Billy's knee. "Sure," he said gently. "Go on."

"The next night. I had old Charley ready. You know old Charley?"

Bud nodded. "I know him."

"I couldn't keep up with Lilah's mare. She rides a good one."

Bud wanted to yell, "Get on with it," but he held the words. Just telling about this was agitating Billy. There was no sense upsetting him more.

"I knew the direction she took," Billy said slowly. "She rode east. The country in that direction turns awful poor. After a few miles I was pretty sure where she was going. I never caught up with her, but a couple of times from a high point, I caught sight of her."

Bud felt as though he would explode. My God, couldn't the kid hurry up? He showed good control by merely saying, "Yes?"

"I figured out where she was going before she got there," Billy said. The tone of his voice showed how pleased he was with himself, but again there was that long silence as though he argued with himself whether or not to go on.

Bud couldn't stand the strain any longer. "What place is that?"

"The old Grimes' place. I don't know if you know it or not."

Bud shook his head. The name was new to him. "Does this Grimes come into town often?"

Billy cackled with amusement. "That would sure give

the town something to talk about. Old Grimes has been
dead a lot of years. The house is a ruin. I don't know
what holds it up."

That jolted Bud to alertness. "Why would Lilah want to
go out to such a place?"

"That's what I kept asking myself all the way there. It'd
be a good place to hide something. Almost nobody ever
goes out that way anymore."

The stiffness froze Bud's face again. "You're going to
have to say it plainer, Billy. I'm not following you at all."

"I'm getting to it," Billy said impatiently. "When I got
to the old house, I thought I'd guessed wrong. I didn't see
her horse. I left old Charley out near the road and went in
on foot. That house gave me the creeps—no light of any
kind in it. I moved around to the back, and I *wasn't*
wrong. There was Lilah's horse tied there."

Bud's hands bunched until the bones ached. "Why did
she go there?" His voice was so cold it was unnatural.

"How would I know?" Billy yelped. "I didn't dare go
barging in."

Bud let his hand rest lightly on Billy's shoulder. "Of
course not," he agreed. "What happened then?"

"Nothing for a long time. I just sat watching that house
till my bones got to aching."

"You never saw any light?"

"All the windows had been broken, but there was one in
the back that looked as though it had been covered with
something. I got the feeling there was some kind of light
behind it, but I couldn't swear to it."

"Maybe a lamp behind a blanket," Bud said thoughtfully. "Sounds like somebody is really anxious to hide
something."

"My guess exactly," Billy agreed. "I thought she would
never come out, then she finally appeared." He hesitated;
Lord, how he dreaded telling Bud this.

"Go on," Bud prompted.

"She wasn't alone," Billy said. "The moonlight was
bright enough for me to see pretty good. A big man was
with her, a bearded man."

Bud felt as though he had been kicked in the stomach.

The only man he knew around here who fitted that description was Toby. But not Toby and Lilah! He groaned
at the thought. "You didn't hear any names?" he asked
harshly.

Billy shook his head. "But she knew him pretty good.
She threw her arms about him and hugged him long and
hard. She kissed him as though she was starving. I didn't
want to tell you this, Marshal, but I thought you should
know."

Bud sat there as though he was frozen. He stared across
the street, his eyes blank. Lilah couldn't have a part in
what Billy had just related. He groaned softly as he
remembered the promise in those warm lips. He wasn't
doubting Billy; it had happened. But damn it, why did it
have to take this turn?

He shook himself as though he was slowly coming back
to life. "I'm glad you told me, Billy. A man gets to believing something because he wants it so badly. Then everything blows up in his face. You did real good in believing
this was important to me."

His voice was so dead it scared Billy. "What are you going to do now?"

"Wait until dark, then ride out there and see who's living in that house."

"Can I go with you, Marshal?"

"I need you to lead me to that place," Bud answered in
a harsh, grim undertone.

"I'll go and get old Charley," Billy said. "What time
shall I be here?"

"Maybe I'd better go with you. I don't want to be seen
around town until I get a few things settled," Bud answered.

Elmer was absorbed in splitting logs into convenient
sizes for firewood, and didn't even see Bud and Billy ar-
rive. He was so wrapped up in his task that he was oblivi-
ous to everything.

Bud looked at the growing pile of firewood. This was
the tag end of summer—a long way to wood-burning
time—and he wondered why Elmer was working so hard.

His shirt was off, and his massive muscles bunched with each stroke. His face dripped sweat. Most men would be lolling in the shade with some kind of a cold drink in their hand.

"Hello, Elmer," he called.

The greeting broke up a backstroke, breaking into Elmer's concentration. The ax blade buried itself in the ground beside the log. Elmer whirled, his face momentarily angry. The anger disappeared when he saw Billy behind Bud. "Is he in some kind of trouble, Marshal?"

"This boy? Not a chance. With his instincts, I think he's going to be a good lawman when he grows up. He's doing something special for me." Bud shook his head, the gesture barely perceptible. Billy caught the admonition not to say anything, and he remained silent.

Elmer's anxiety vanished, and he said heartily, "I'm glad to hear that. A man never knows what mischief a boy can get into. You got time to slide down and have a cooling drink?"

"I've got until nightfall," Bud replied. "Nothing would suit me better."

"I'll be right back," Elmer said and disappeared around the house. He reappeared, carrying a jug wrapped in a gunny bag. "Keep it in the shade," he explained. "The shade's better on that side."

Bud hoped it wasn't an offer of an alcoholic drink. His face cleared as he saw Elmer pour a cup of water.

"I'll bet you thought it was beer or something," the older man said and chuckled.

"The thought ran across my mind," Bud said, and drank in long gulps. The water wasn't cold, but it was cool enough to be acceptable. He extended his cup for a refill, then drank more slowly. "That goes good on this kind of a day." Curiosity finally overcame him, and he asked, "Isn't this an awfully hot job for a day like this?"

Elmer finished his cup of water before he answered. "It is," he replied. "But it's better than cutting wood on a cold day. You have to bundle up so much that it's hard to stir around. I'm an odd-job man, and most of my work seems to come in the winter time. I get a lot of wood cutting."

He grinned. "If I'm going to cut wood, I'd rather do it when I'm paid for it."

Bud nodded. That made sense to him. He stretched out and cupped his hands behind his head.

"I'd like to get a regular job," Elmer said. "It'd give me something I could depend on. But it's hard to find such a job in a small town like this."

Bud bobbed his head. He could understand what Elmer was saying. Making a living came hard for some men. "Maybe that job will come along before you know it."

"I hope so," Elmer grumbled. "You're not taking Billy into something dangerous?"

"You know better than that," Bud retorted.

The shortness of the reply didn't wipe away Elmer's humor. "I just thought I'd ask. Billy can be venturesome at times."

"I'll keep an eye on him."

"That's all I wanted to hear," Elmer said easily. He, too, stretched out on the ground. "I'm going to grab a wink before I go back to work."

"A sound idea," Bud approved. He was more tired than he realized, for his eyes slowly closed. The last thing he remembered was that Elmer started to ask him something.

Billy looked at the two sleeping men. God, he thought in disgust, they must be getting old to fall asleep like this. He had noted that the older a man got the easier he slipped into slumber.

Elmer shook Bud awake. He grinned down at Bud and said, "Supper time. You must've needed that nap."

Bud sat up and rubbed the remnants of sleep from his eyes. "I guess I did," he admitted.

He washed up at the bench outside the house. The towel hanging from the peg was fairly clean. The food was plain but good. For a lone man, Elmer ran a remarkably efficient household.

Bud spooned up a bite of beans. "You're lucky to have Elmer, Billy."

Later, he offered to help with the dishes. He knew that was the only offer he could make to pay for his meal.

"Billy can do that," Elmer said.

"But I want to," Bud insisted.

"Billy gets out of too many chores." He frowned at the boy. "Get that grin off your face. You may get by this time, but I'll only double up on you."

Billy grimaced. "He will, too."

Elmer was humming as he washed the dishes. Bud knew this was a happy, little family. He needn't worry about them. But just the same, he wished he could do something solid for Elmer. It couldn't be anything that smelled of charity; Elmer would fiercely reject an offer like that.

They sat out before the small house, smoking. Bud rolled a cigarette, and Elmer puffed on a corncob pipe, battered from use. He smoked a rough-smelling tobacco. If Bud had to use that tobacco, it would knock him out.

Bud didn't move until the darkness creeping up from the earth had darkened the skies and brightened the stars. "I guess we'd better go, Billy," he said. "You'd better get Charley ready."

Billy jumped to his feet and dashed toward the ramshackle shed.

"Wish I could afford a horse for him," Elmer said regretfully. "But you know how things are."

"Sure," Bud said easily. "But you're not depriving him of a thing. He's a lucky kid. He's got everything he needs."

Billy came back with the donkey, and the animal resisted every tug on his reins. "Come on, you hammerhead," Billy said wrathfully. "Sometimes I get so mad at his stubborness! Look at him. He's not much up against Lucky."

Bud didn't give him any sympathy. "He sure beats walking."

The wrath slipped off of Billy's face. He tweaked Charley's ear. "I guess he does at that."

Bud mounted, then leaned down to shake hands with Elmer. "Thanks for as good a meal as I've had in a long time. Don't worry, I'll keep an eye on Billy. I wouldn't put him in any danger." He winced a little at the firm handshake. Elmer had a hell of a grip.

"I know it," Elmer said comfortably.

Bud looked back after fifty yards. Elmer still stood there, watching them. Maybe Billy didn't have all the material things, but he was still one lucky kid. He would do some positive thinking about doing something for the two.

Chapter 19

It seemed as though it was taking forever for them to reach the old Grimes' place. "How much farther, Billy?"

The boy knew the country well. He squinted at a huge, lightning-blasted oak and said, "Not more than a couple of miles."

"I hope not," Bud muttered. Thinking of Lilah had dissipated all the peace he had gathered this afternoon. How deeply was Lilah tied up in this mess? He groaned at the possibility of her being in too deep. No, he thought angrily, she can't be. But she might be tied up with Toby, and if she's connected with him in any way, she *is* in over her head.

He rode with the black thoughts enveloping him. If Lilah was involved, he wanted to get this over as quickly as possible.

He started to ask Billy again how much farther it was when Billy said, "There it is. To your right."

Bud jerked his head that way. The cloudy skies made the night dark, and the old, weather-beaten house was hard to pick out as his eyes adjusted to what light there was. He sat scowling at the miserable place. It was too far away for him to pick out details plainly, but he knew the closer he got to it, the poorer it would look.

"She came out to this place?" he asked incredulously.

"I followed her here."

Bud caught the stubbornness in Billy's voice and said hastily, "I'm not doubting you, Billy. But in God's name, why?"

Billy shrugged. "I told you about the man. She came out here to see him."

That was the only logical explanation, and he wanted to reject it. He wanted to ask Billy if he thought the big, bearded man was still here, but there was no way Billy could know that. "We better leave Lucky and Charley here," he said in a hard voice. "You come around with me to show me the back of the house, then you scoot back here as fast as you can."

Billy opened his mouth to protest, and Bud felt his disappointment. "I want you to keep a close eye on Lucky and Charley. Maybe I'll have to use Lucky in a hurry. I don't know what I'll dig up. Besides, I promised your pa I'd keep you out of harm."

"But maybe I could be of some help to you."

"How? With your bare hands? No, you'll do exactly as I say."

They made a wide swing of the house, and Bud could see no evidence of life in it. Up close, the house looked even worse. This old relic didn't have much longer to stand.

Billy pulled at Bud's arm. "There," he whispered. "There's the door I saw them come out of." He pointed to an indefinite blob.

"You could see on a night like this?"

Billy bristled at the skepticism in Bud's voice. "It wasn't like tonight. The moon was bright. I'm telling you I could see."

"Sure," Bud said quietly. He knew what he was doing. He was only seeking any excuse that might free Lilah of his blame. "I believe it happened just like you said." He squeezed Billy's shoulder. "Now get on back to Lucky and Charley as fast as you can. Don't run," he added as an afterthought. "Somebody might hear you. Work your way back carefully."

Billy was still rebellious, and every few steps he stopped and looked back. Each time, Bud waved him on.

It grew very silent after Billy left. One of the night animals made a rustling sound in the brush behind Bud, and he started at the sound. Somewhere in the trees surrounding the house, an owl hooted derisively at him. Maybe it wasn't actually at him, but it sounded that way.

He thought he'd better stand to relieve his cramped muscles and started to rise. The creaking of the door hinges quelled his motion. Instantly, Bud sank back to the ground. The door was opening, and Bud could see light in the room. A lamp burned there, and whatever was at the window masked it.

A man was momentarily silhouetted in the doorway, then he stepped out into the darkness. The door was immediately closed behind him. There was at least one other person in that room.

The man walked some fifty feet to the wreck of a small building. He wrestled with the sagging hinges of the outhouse door, cursing it softly. Then he disappeared.

Bud hunkered closer to the ground. He could make no move until that man reappeared and went back in the house. He felt an insect crawl over his hand, and he slapped at it, careful to make the slap light. Finally he heard those rusty hinges squeak again. The man came out and walked back to the house, pausing to light a cigarette. The small flame briefly illuminated his face, and Bud saw he was clean-shaven.

That brief glimpse told him two things: it wasn't Toby, and there were at least two men here, maybe more. Five men had driven the Kaiser horses to Texas. He didn't like the thought of those odds, but there wasn't much he could do about it. If he waited another day to gather help, the people in that house could leave, and he might never catch up with them.

His teeth were bared as he drew his pistol. He had one big advantage in his favor—surprise. He was ready for trouble, and they were not. He eased up to the door, alert for any alien sound that might warn him that he was being watched. He heard nothing disturbing and started to reach for the door knob when something occurred to him. Hadn't he heard these hinges creak when the man came out? He impatiently shook his head. He couldn't remember, but he couldn't take the risk that his memory was incorrect. If the hinges did creak, it could be advance warning to the men inside.

If he was going to give them a surprise, it might as well be a complete one. He gripped his gun harder, lowered a shoulder, and rammed against the door. It was old and flimsy and literally shattered before the force he put against it. His momentum carried him into the room, and he lost his balance. He lit on a shoulder and rolled. He came to a halt against the farthest wall, and his surprise was complete. He leveled his pistol at three gaping faces. All were armed, but none had made a move toward his gun. One of them was Toby.

"Just hold it where you are," Bud said, gesturing with the gun to give the words greater emphasis.

He didn't like the way the men were spaced. One man stood near Toby, but the second one was across the room, standing near a window. If it came down to gunplay, Bud felt he could take care of Toby and the man beside him. But the third would have more time than they did, and that extra second or two could make it difficult.

Toby stared at him, blank surprise molding his face. "What the hell are you doing, busting in here?" he blustered.

"I think you know," Bud snapped. "All three of you are under arrest."

That announcement pulled the skin around Toby's eyes taut. "For what?" he demanded. "We ain't done nothing."

"I think you have," Bud said, "like taking Kaiser's horses down to Texas and selling them."

He heard the harsh suck of Toby's breath. That had hit him hard.

"Broady is under arrest in Amarillo. I'm taking you three down there so he can identify you."

Toby's eyes were jerking in his head, and his lips were trembling.

"You're crazy," he stammered. "You ain't got no proof."

"I have all I need," Bud said calmly. "Unbuckle those

gun belts and drop them on the floor." His eyes were narrow and alert as he watched three sets of fingers fumble
with the belt buckles. He caught the betraying movement
of Toby's hands and cried sharply, "Don't be a damned
fool, Toby. Don't do it."

But desperation was driving Toby, and no mere words
could have stopped him. He grabbed for the butt of his
gun and jerked. It wasn't a smooth motion—he had never
been good with a gun.

The second man had followed Toby's motion, and Bud
could give them no further time. His sights centered on
Toby's belly, and he pulled the trigger. The impact of the
bullet knocked Toby back a good pace, and he looked at
his killer from an agonized face.

Bud didn't watch him fall; he had other work to do. He
swung the pistol barrel and covered the second man. This
one wasn't bad, for his gun was lifting out of its holster.
He fired again, and the bullet plowed into the man's chest.
His face turned slack and there was a loosening all over
his figure.

Bud switched his attention to the third man. This one
was the most dangerous as he had more time to draw. Bud
wouldn't be surprised to find himself staring down a gun
barrel.

But the man wasn't standing there. He had turned and
was diving out of the blanketed window. Bud heard the
ripping of material and the crash of the man's body
against the ground.

"Here," he roared. "Hold it!" Rushing to the window,
he heard the pound of running feet, but with the poor
light he couldn't immediately locate the fleeing man. When
he finally picked up the running figure, the man was almost to the fringe of trees that surrounded the house. Bud
fired once, then again. With a marksman's instinct, he
knew both shots missed. Then the running figure was gone,
swallowed up by the trees.

He turned back from the window. He had two men
here to make sure of. He cursed himself for missing, but
the man had reacted quickly.

Bud bent over the man who had been nearest Toby. A

brief inspection told him there was no further concern for this one. His eyes were wide and staring, and they saw nothing.

He moved over to Toby. Toby's face was a ghastly gray, and his breathing was labored.

"Why did you try such a fool stunt, Toby?"

For a moment, he didn't think Toby heard the question, then his eyes slowly fluttered open. They stared at Bud without comprehension. Then his face twisted. "Damn you," he said brokenly. A rush of blood choked him.

Bud waited until the choking paroxysm passed. He hoped Toby would be able to tell a little more. "Didn't you know you couldn't make it?"

Toby's eyes were growing dull, and Bud waited anxiously. "Yes," he acknowledged faintly. "But I couldn't let you take me down to Texas. I wasn't going to spend any time in jail."

His coughing started again, and blood spewed out on the floor. He got control of himself again and gasped. "You ain't won nothing yet. Lilah won't look at you. Not after this."

"I'll deal with Lilah later," Bud said grimly.

A light briefly fired Toby's eyes. "You can't deal with Lilah. She's too smart for you. And you won't marry her. She's my wife." He had raised his head a few inches, and it flopped back against the floor.

Bud straightened wearily. Those were Toby's last words. Bud felt drained and dull—it all seemed such a waste. But he had learned valuable information. Lilah and Toby had been together in this horse-stealing ring. His chest hurt as though he had been smashed a fearful blow. He saw Lilah in his mind. Who would have thought that such a lovely woman could be involved in this mess?

Bud started slowly toward the door. Well, it had happened. As much as he protested, he couldn't change a thing. All he had left was to clean up the last few details.

He stopped short as he heard the pound of running feet. That surely couldn't be the man who had escaped. He wouldn't be that foolish. He stepped quickly outside and pressed against the building, his eyes seeking the runner. He leveled his pistol and waited.

Then he recognized the running figure. It was Billy. All the stress of the last few moments wrapped around him, making him furious. "Billy," he yelled. "What the hell do you think you're doing?"

His intensity scared the boy, for Billy's eyes rolled. "I heard some shots. I thought you might be hurt. I came to see if I could help."

"You could've got your head shot off," Bud snapped. "Don't go in there," he said, as Billy started forward, "unless you want to look at a couple of dead men."

Even in the poor light he could see the shiver that ran through Billy. "Were they the ones you were looking for?" The kid was scared to death, and it was time to alleviate his fear.

"They were." He draped an arm over Billy's shoulders. "You did a hell of a job, leading me out here. The horse-stealing ring is broken." He thought dully of Lilah. It wouldn't be over until he finally arrested *her*.

Billy was still shaking. "There were only two of them?"

"No. One got away. He didn't want any part of the fight. He dove out a window and escaped."

"But you'll find him," Billy persisted.

"Maybe," Bud granted. "Let's get back to Lucky and Charley and get out of here. I want to get you back home."

The farther they got away from the house, the more Billy chattered. "You could have got killed, Bud," he said in awe.

"But I wasn't." Bud wished the kid would shut up. Most of it was over now. He dreaded what lay ahead.

A light was on in the small house when they arrived. Elmer must have heard them coming, for he was outside waiting.

"Damn, I'm glad to see you two," he said. "I had a bad feeling about this night."

"It was bad enough, Pa," Billy said solemnly. "Bud killed two of the horse thieves he was after."

Elmer looked accusingly at Bud, and the lawman shook his head.

"I made sure Billy was in no danger. I left him with Lucky and Charley. There were three of the thieves using the old Grimes' place, and I managed to get two of them. The third got away."

"Did you know him?"

"A complete stranger," Bud answered. "Maybe I'll be able to find him, maybe not. It won't matter. I know the leader of that gang." He was silent for a long moment, then thought better of it. Elmer had a right to know all the ramifications. "It's Lilah," he said simply.

Elmer looked stunned. "That good-looking woman who owns the saloon?"

Bud nodded, his face composed.

"Who would've thought it, Marshal? Such a pretty little thing. Are you sure?"

That dull ache reappeared in Bud's chest. "I'm damned sure. I've got to get to town and arrest her."

Both Elmer and Bud caught the eagerness flooding Billy's face. They answered at the same time: "You're not going." The disappointment in Billy's face didn't soften either of them.

"You've done enough, Billy," Bud said, trying to ease the kid's disappointment. "Without you, I wouldn't have been able to catch those thieves."

Chapter 20

The horses were tethered better than five hundred yards from the house, and Cass ran every foot of the way. His lungs were on fire, and he had to fight for every breath. He didn't dare stop; he didn't know whether or not the marshal was right behind him. He had heard talk about the marshal's speed, and he had seen it with his own eyes. God, it was unbelievable. He was smart to have run for it, or he could have wound up like Toby and Gabe. He knew both of them were dead. He had seen the way they fell, the way they sprawled. No man ever recovered after being hit like that.

His hands were shaking as he untied his horse, and for a moment that step up into the stirrup seemed insurmountable. But he made it, whirled the horse, and looked behind him. He saw nothing, heard nothing. A whimpering sound escaped his throat. Oh God, he had made it. How in the hell had the marshal found the Grimes' place?

Cass knew one thing for sure: That damned marshal had busted their horse-thieving ring all to hell. He'd better get out of this country fast. He debated briefly on a troublesome thought before he made his decision. He knew he was ahead of the marshal, and Carson would spend a little time with the two bodies. Cass had the advantage of time if he wanted to stop at Lilah's place. He could make it short, and it would give her a chance to get out of the country.

He sank his spurs deep. He mustn't be careless and let time slip away from him. He would stop at the saloon only long enough to run in and back out.

"The miserable son-of-a-bitch," he said aloud savagely. "He sure ruined everything."

By the number of horses tied before the saloon, Lilah was doing a thriving business tonight. Cass hesitated only a moment, then set his jaw and dashed into the saloon. Lilah was talking to three men at the far end of the bar. Cass kept beckoning to her, and with each passing second his gestures grew more frantic.

"Lilah," the tall, lean man said, "do you know him?"

She turned her head to follow his directing finger. He face went tight, and she said a sharp. "No."

"Well, he sure acts like he wants to talk to you."

"I'd better go and see what he wants." Lilah tried to say it lightly. A warning bell was clanging in her head, and her stomach felt as though it was tied in knots.

She approached Cass, her face hard. "Haven't I told you not to come in here?"

"I had to tell you this." Cass's expression was apologetic. "That marshal found the old house tonight. He broke in the door and took Toby, Gabe, and me by surprise. He had a gun on us, and warned us not to make any foolish moves. He said he was taking all of us down to Texas so that Broady could identify us. Lilah, he traced those horses and found out who rustled them. Toby ignored his warning. He tried to draw, and so did Gabe. The marshal shot Toby before he got his gun out. Gabe did better, but he didn't have enough time to pull a trigger." He shook his head in amazement. "I've seen some fast men, but never anybody faster than that marshal."

Lilah's face had gone white and stark. She looked as though she would be screaming at any instant. "Didn't you try to do anything?" she whispered in a strained voice.

"You damned right I did. I dove out of a window. He even took a couple of shots at me. I was lucky. He missed."

Lilah's fingers were bent and rigid. They looked as though they were ready to rend and tear. "You didn't stop to see if you could do anything for Toby and Gabe?"

Cass looked at her with mild surprise. "I saw the way they fell, like grain sacks that suddenly got big rips in them. I knew I couldn't do anything for them, so I got out of there as fast as I could." His face had turned mean at her criticism. "And I'm doing something else. I'm getting out of this country as fast as I can. I wouldn't be surprised to see the marshal come roaring in any minute now. If you're smart, you'll take my advice and get out, too."

There was a vast hollow where Lilah's stomach should be. Only one thought was in her head: Toby was dead. The thought hammered over and over in an evil refrain.

She wanted to weep and rave, and her composure amazed her. "All right, Cass," she said dully. "You've told me."

Cass looked at Lilah with worried eyes. If he ever saw a woman close to cracking up, here was one. There was no telling what a mad woman would do. He'd better get out of here while the getting was good. "Good luck, Lilah," he said huskily. As an afterthought, he added, "Take good care of yourself."

Lilah nodded jerkily, but Cass wasn't sure she fully understood what he said. He touched the brim of his hat, turned, and hurried out of the door. He was damned glad to be out of there. He wouldn't breathe easy until this town was far behind him.

Lilah didn't move until Cass disappeared, then she tried to get herself together. But that horrible refrain wouldn't leave her mind. Toby was dead; she would never see him again. Her hands hurt, and she looked down at them. They were so tightly clenched that the nails bit into her palms.

Something Cass said echoed in her mind. He was getting out of town, and he had said she'd better do the same thing. It was sound advice. She didn't know how much Bud knew, but if he had unraveled this much of the puzzle, he was probably aware of her part in the ring. He would come straight to the saloon. She couldn't stay here and wait for him.

She called Butch over to her and said in a brittle voice, "Take care of things, Butch."

He looked curiously at her. This wasn't the Lilah he knew. Something was drastically wrong. "You all right, Lilah?"

She looked at him with wide-open eyes, and he had never seen such pools of despair. "Am I paying you to ask questions?"

"No," he said meekly. This was a wild woman, close to going over the edge. He had one other question, and he was going to ask it, even if it loosed all her wrath upon him.

"How long do you think you'll be gone?"

Her eyes blazed at him. "As long as it takes me to finish a job that has to be done. You keep running things until you hear from me."

She came around the end of the bar, and her heels beat out a rapid staccato against the floor. She had to go to her quarters and get a gun, then wait until Bud returned to town.

Butch watched her go. He didn't know what she had in mind, but he was damned glad he wasn't the object of her fury.

Bud had no idea what time it was when he rode into Chandler, and there was no moon or stars to help him. He had a feeling it was getting late, probably close to midnight.

All the way there, he had been turning over in his mind what he was going to say to Lilah. He was afraid his personal feeling would weaken him, and he would babble like a baby. No, he thought, his jaw set. There was no sense trying to make it easier for her. He would simply announce that she was under arrest for horse stealing.

He looked at the horses tethered outside the saloon, and he winced. Lilah was doing an excellent business. Why did she have to steal horses?

He dismounted slowly, secured Lucky and walked into

the saloon. A lot of people recognized him immediately, for the babble of conversation ceased. Bud smiled bleakly as he felt the uneasiness steal through the room. Nix was right when he said establish your reputation fast—it'll make things a lot easier for you. Killing three men had done that for Bud. After tonight, he supposed his reputation would grow even more, but he didn't want or need a reputation anymore. He wanted to leave Chandler and forget it existed.

Lilah wasn't behind the bar. The big floorman she occasionally used was there instead. Bud walked up to him. He didn't know the man's name, though he had seen him several times before. But the man knew who he was, for there was respect in his eyes. He tried to meet Bud's look and failed.

Bud gripped the edge of the bar. "Where's Lilah?"

"She's out—" the man started.

Bud was too weary to take any smart talk. He reached over the bar and seized the man by his shirt, putting pressure on the man's throat. "Don't smart mouth me. I can see she isn't here. Where is she?"

The material twisting against Butch's throat was beginnign to cut off his air, for his face was darkening. He resented this handling, but he didn't dare do anything about it. He licked his lips and said. "She went out. That's all." There was a desperate tone to the words. He thought the marshal didn't like the answer, for Bud's eyes seemed to flash fire. "I wouldn't be back here if she wasn't out, would I?"

Bud momentarily considered that. That was a logical answer. Except in a rush, Lilah took care of the bar alone. "Where did she go?"

Butch licked his lips again. Those eyes were so damned merciless. "I don't know," he said frantically. "Look, she doesn't tell me where she's going. She doesn't have to. I only work for her."

Bud nodded slowly as he let go of the man. He had no fault with that logic, either. "If she comes in, don't say anything about me being here."

He took a half step away from the bar, then turned as a

thought struck him. Butch cringed as he saw that purposeful face. Oh Lord, the marshal didn't like something he had said.

"Her quarters are up over the saloon, aren't they?"

Butch nodded carefully.

"Is she up there?"

"I wouldn't know." How those eyes burned into him! He would sure hate to be caught telling this marshal a lie.

Bud was somewhat mollified, for he nodded and said, "Okay." He turned and walked out of the saloon.

Butch didn't draw a free breath until Bud was out of sight.

He hesitated a moment outside, trying to lay out his course. Had Lilah got wind of what had happened tonight? That was possible. Bud thought of the third man diving through the window. That man might have risked coming into town to warn her. He pounded a fist into a palm. God, he wished he knew where she was. He wanted to get this over with.

He passed the corner of the saloon and glanced at the outside stairs leading to Lilah's quarters. Bounding up them, he tried the door. It was locked.

He stood a moment in indecision. Ordinarily, the thought of breaking into her private living quarters would have been repulsive to him, but that feeling was gone now. Lilah was a criminal; she had lost all rights or privileges.

Bud put his shoulder against the door and pushed with all his strength. The door was flimsy, and the lock wasn't the stoutest. He heard a sharp, crackling sound, and the door gave suddenly. He almost lost his balance, and it took a couple of stumbling steps for him to regain it.

He looked slowly about the room. This was the first time he had been in here. He looked at the bed, and the sight brought back the aching hurt. He had dreamed of sharing that bed with Lilah. He smelled the subtle fragrance of the perfume she wore. God, how he hurt. Why did it have to turn out this way?

He pulled back a curtain which protected her clothes in a small nook. The same sweet smell was in there too. He pawed through them, trying to determine if she had taken some of them with her, but he couldn't be sure.

He found two valises in the second room, and that surely told him something. If she had fled, wouldn't she have taken her clothes? He nodded. She hadn't left Chandler. She was somewhere in town.

He went out the door, trying to close it behind him. It was splintered, and he couldn't completely shut it. He arranged it as best as he could and left it that way. It didn't matter—Lilah wouldn't be spending much time there anymore.

He went down the flight of stairs, and his footsteps were dragging. All he could think to do was to go back to his office and wait out the rest of the long night. If he heard any news about Lilah, he would go out and pick her up.

He reached his office and fumbled in his pocket for the key. He was reaching to open the door when a voice behind him said, "Hold it right there, Bud. There's a gun centered on the middle of your back."

He knew that voice; he knew it too well. "Lilah, I've been looking for you. You're under arrest."

Her shrill burst of laughter was too high-pitched. "You poor damn fool. Didn't you hear what I said? I've got a gun trained on the middle of your back. One wrong move, and I'll use it. It all depends on how long you trail out the last few moments of your life."

Bud kept his hands carefully raised. By the tone of her voice, there was no doubt he was dealing with a hysterical woman. The slightest wrong move, and she would shoot him in the back. Maybe some conversation would prolong the moment.

"You sound different, Lilah," he said softly. "What happened to change you? Not too long ago, I thought we meant something to each other."

She cursed him with every foul word she knew. His face hardened as he listened. She didn't miss a one. Finally, she ran out of breath and paused. "That was before you killed Toby. Why did you do it?"

"He was a horse thief, Lilah," he said calmly. "It was my job."

That started her on a new tirade, thoroughly mixed with expletives and obscenities. "Toby was my man. We were married."

Bud winced at the confirmation of Toby's disclosure, and his back muscles tightened. At any second now she was going to shoot, and there was nothing he could do about it.

She was crying now, and it was making her voice jerky. "He was the only man I ever cared for. You spoiled that."

Now, he thought, and braced himself for the shock of the bullet. It didn't come, and he imagined she was enjoying baiting him. "You could have done a lot better, Lilah. You know I was interested in you. I wanted to marry you."

"You?" she said scornfully. She broke into shrill laughter, laughter that was almost lewd. "I only said I was interested to keep you occupied. After knowing Toby, do you think I could let you touch me?"

Bud winced. Her words were cutting him to pieces. He managed to keep his voice even. "You didn't even give me a chance, Lilah."

"I gave you all you're going to get from me. I'm giving you these few moments to let you know why I'm going to kill you!"

Bud was angered at his own impotence, and he said furiously, "Go ahead, Lilah. Get it over with."

"I want to see you squirm a little more, Mr. Big Man. You thought everything was going your way. This will show you how wrong you were."

"Lilah," a new voice said, "there's a scatter-gun leveled at your back. Drop that gun, or I'll blow you apart."

Bud heard Lilah gasp. That was Elmer talking. How had he managed to slip up behind her? Would his threat mean anything to her? It all depended how far her desperation would drive her. Maybe she had reached the point where life was no longer important to her.

"I mean what I say, Lilah," Elmer said in a low, grating voice. "My patience is running thin. If you want to live, drop that gun."

Bud heard the click of a hammer being cocked. It was surprising how a small sound could carry so well.

"I just cocked the second hammer," Elmer said, and there was a new, harsh urgency in his voice. "Do you know what both barrels will do to a pretty woman? She won't be pretty anymore."

Elmer had drawn a brutal picture, and it must have reached her, for she gave a little cry of despair and dropped her gun. Bud heard its thud as it hit the walk.

"It's done, Bud," Elmer said, and there was a weariness in his voice.

Bud turned. Lilah had her face buried in her hands. Her moaning shook her shoulders. She sounded like an animal in mortal pain. He pulled a pair of handcuffs from his hip pocket and clamped them around her wrists. Her sobbing never ceased. He wondered if this ugly little incident had pushed her over the edge of sanity.

Bud tugged gently on the handcuffs and led her into the office. He pushed her down into his chair behind the desk, took one cuff off, and then reclicked it over the arm of the chair. He looked briefly at her. Her crying had wiped all beauty from her face. Her mouth was open with her sobbing, and her eyes were puffy and swollen.

He shook his head and moved to the front of the office where Elmer stood "How in the hell did you get here?"

Elmer chuckled low in his throat. "I listened to what you told me when you came home with Billy—particularly that part about Toby being her man. When a woman suffers that kind of a loss, she can go crazy." He shook his head, then added thoughtfully, "She almost did."

"How well I know that," Bud said solemnly. "I was sweating gallons. At any moment, I expected her to shoot."

"Not a very pleasant spot to be in," Elmer agreed. "I came in town right after you did, then I saw you come out of the saloon. By your looks, I knew Lilah wasn't there. I saw you climb up the stairs, then come back down. You looked like a sleepwalker, so I thought I'd better keep an eye on you. I stayed a good distance behind you, then saw Lilah come out of the shadows. Both of you looked unnatural, and I figured something was going on. I slipped up behind her and heard enough to know what had happened. I never heard so much hatred in a woman's voice. She sounded plumb crazy.

"I didn't see the gun, but I knew she had one. The big problem I faced was stopping her before she pulled the trigger. I gave her a personal threat to think about. What I promised her would shake any vain woman. They all have a degree of that." His grin broadened. "It worked."

"You did just fine," Bud said fervently. "Elmer, do you know how much I owe you?"

"Just a small repayment for what you did for Billy," Elmer said easily. "You pointed that boy straight. Maybe it marks the account paid."

"It sure does," Bud said, and wrung Elmer's hand.

"What are you going to do with her?" Elmer asked curiously. "There's no jail here. Somebody might try to free her. Didn't she have quite a bunch working for her?"

"Five that I know of," Bud frowned. "I don't think any of them would try, but it could happen. I'll sit up all night and watch her, then I'll take her by stage to Guthrie. They have facilities there to take care of her."

"What will happen then?"

"She'll be tried, and if it turns out like it should, she'll be imprisoned."

Elmer was shaking his head, and Bud asked, "You don't believe that?"

Elmer laughed. "Oh, I believe she'll be tried. She'll get a good lawyer, and he'll get her free. There's not much solid proof against her, is there?"

"Not much," Bud admitted. "About all I've got are the few words Toby said before he died. Unless the rest of her gang is arrested—" He broke off and shrugged.

"That's a beautiful woman going up before a male jury. Do you think they'll convict her?"

A frown etched itself deep into Bud's forehead. Elmer was putting some disturbing thoughts in his head. If Lilah was freed, and that was entirely possible, what would happen because of that insane hatred she showed before El-

mer stopped her? A little shiver ran through him. Would
he still be willing to go after her?

"Elmer, isn't there a stage to Guthrie in the morning?"

"Sure is," Elmer replied. "About ten o'clock."

"We'll be on it," Bud said firmly.

He looked back at Lilah. The broken sounds of crying
no longer came from her. He'd be glad when morning
came.

"You better get on home and grab some sleep, Elmer."

Elmer shook his head firmly. "I'm staying right here. It
won't be any harder on me than on you. It'll let you move
around a little. Don't underestimate her, Bud. She's one
dangerous woman. I know if she was as mad at me as she
is at you, I'd be afraid to close my eyes. Don't argue. My
mind is made up."

It would be comfortable to have Elmer here, Bud
thought. He wouldn't have to worry about Lilah attempt-
ing an escape. He wouldn't have to worry about closing
his eyes for a brief sleep. "I appreciate it, Elmer."

"Oh Lord," Elmer said in mock disgust, "here comes
that sickening thanks again."

Chapter 21

Bud opened his eyes and stared groggily about him. He had no idea what time it was, nor did he immediately know his location. He hadn't been asleep very long, or if he had, it hadn't done him much good. He felt as though he had been run over by a stampeding herd, and he ached in every bone. Then comprehension flooded in on him. He was in his own office, and he had gotten his sleep by stretching out on the floor. No wonder he ached so.

He looked to his right, and Elmer sat on the floor a couple of paces from him. He was awake, for he winked at Bud.

"How are you feeling?" Elmer asked.

"I hope I never feel any worse. Any trouble?"

"Quiet as a graveyard," Elmer replied. His eyes flicked to Lilah. "She's been asleep the last couple of hours. Her conscience sure wasn't bothering her any."

Bud looked at Lilah. She slept slumped in the chair, and he heard the soft bubbling of her breathing. With sleep masking her wildness, she looked almost pretty again. He quickly erased that weakening feeling. This was the same woman who not too long ago would have delighted in blowing his backbone apart.

He looked back at Elmer. "You got a watch?"

Elmer nodded and pulled out a tarnished watch as big

as a turnip. "It's about six o'clock, if that's what you're asking about."

Bud groaned. Four more hours until the stage came through. As battered as his body felt, he didn't think he could stand the wait, nor the coach ride. "I'm going out, Elmer. Keep a close eye on her."

"I'll do that. Some important business?"

"If I'm going on the stage, I sure can't take my horse," Bud said wearily. "I've got to make arrangements for him. I'll stop by and get a bite to eat. Are you hungry?"

"A little," Elmer replied. "Most of all, I could stand some coffee."

"I'll be back as soon as I can, Elmer."

Bud kept stretching his muscles as he stepped outdoors. He felt as though last night had aged him twenty years. He went first to the livery stable, and Little was just stirring around. He moved stiffly, and said, "Didn't sleep very well last night. I ache all over."

"Tell me about it," Bud said sardonically. "Sam, I've got to make the stage at ten o'clock. I'm escorting a prisoner to Guthrie."

"Is that Lilah?" Little asked curiously. "I heard something about you arresting her last night."

Bud sighed. Damn, how news traveled in a small town. "That's right. She was the head of a ring stealing horses."

Little shook his head. "It's hard to believe such a good-looking woman would be tied up in something like that. What do you suppose drove her to it?"

"She wanted the money, I guess," Bud replied soberly. He didn't want to talk about Lilah, nor even think about her. "Sam, can you have Lucky saddled and at my office about nine forty-five, no later?" He reached in his pocket for a five-dollar bill. "That takes care of my bill. The rest is yours."

Little's face brightened as he pocketed the bill. "I can do that." He was still curious. "If you're leaving on the stage, why do you want your horse?"

"I've got something in mind to do with him. Don't be late."

"I'll be there," Sam promised again.

Bud stopped next at a restaurant. He ordered three ham sandwiches and three cups of coffee. "Make those sandwiches thick," he ordered.

A woman wrapped the sandwiches for him and placed them and the coffee into a big paper sack. "I really appreciate this," Bud said, and paid her. It was funny. Almost his last contact with this town was pleasant.

He walked back to the office, stopped before Elmer, and handed him a sandwich and a container of coffee.

Elmer sniffed at the aroma of both. "I just changed my mind. I'm *very* hungry."

"Good," Bud replied. He wished he could say the same thing. He walked back to the chair Lilah was in and placed a sandwich and coffee before her.

She looked at him with veiled eyes, and he couldn't read the emotion behind them. He wondered if she hated him as much as she had earlier.

"I'm not hungry," she said flatly.

"Better eat something," Bud advised her. "It's a long trip to Guthrie. You'll be pretty empty before we get there."

She tried to lift a manacled hand, and the chair stopped her. "I can't eat very well like this."

He unlocked both cuffs and warned, "You be careful, Lilah."

She gave him a mocking smile. "How could I be otherwise?"

Bud went back and sat down beside Elmer. He kept his eyes on Lilah. Desperation could drive a person to unpredictable action, but she seemed intent only on eating and drinking. She would nibble at the sandwich, then swallow a mouthful of coffee. Bud kept reminding himself she was only a prisoner with no more privileges or rights than any other prisoner. But it was hard to watch and keep his mind cold against her.

Elmer finished his sandwich and gulped down the rest of the coffee. "Good," he rumbled. "Wish you'd doubled the order."

Bud handed over his sandwich. He had taken only one small bite from the corner. The food stuck in his throat, and it was hard to get down. "Have mine. I only took a small bite out of it."

"You sure?" Elmer asked, but he was already reaching eagerly for it. The bite taken out of it didn't bother him. Elmer was a big man, and he needed a lot of fuel.

He hadn't finished when a voice called from the door. "Marshal! You in there?"

Bud sighed. He would know that voice anyplace. "I'm here, Mayor," he answered.

Crump came in, his small black eyes sparkling. "I heard you did something noteworthy last night. I heard you arrested that woman."

He hadn't seen Lilah farther back in the narrow room, and Bud frowned at him. He wished Crump would keep his voice down. Lilah had already suffered enough humiliation.

"I did," he said softly. "That horse-stealing ring is broken."

"Ain't that fine?" Crump crowed. "Remember what I told you about that woman? I said she was no good. There's an old saying that goes 'the female is the deadlier of the species.' It's sure true, isn't it?"

"Shut up," Bud thundered. He jerked his head in Lilah's direction.

Crump looked that way and gaped foolishly. "I ain't taking nothing back," he said belligerently. "You young bucks think we old-timers don't know nothing. What are you going to do with her?"

"I'm taking her to Guthrie to face charges there," Bud said coldly.

Crump rubbed his hands together. "You did one hell of a job here. I'm going to write and tell your boss so."

"Don't bother," Bud said, his voice growing more frozen. He had had a belly-full of this fussy, crabby little man, and that included Crump's town. Nix would give him a new assignment. If he refused, Bud would simply turn in his badge. "I'm not coming back," he finished.

Crump stared at him, his face growing gray as he realized what Bud was saying. "You can't do that," Crump squalled. "That would leave my town without protection of any kind."

"Hire yourself a sheriff," Bud said indifferently.

Crump was really suffering. "I tried that before. It didn't work."

Bud shrugged. "You hired the wrong men. You should be looking for somebody like Elmer."

Crump looked at Elmer with disfavor. "He hasn't the right qualifications."

"You're wrong," Bud snapped. He thought of Elmer's intervention last night. "He's tough, resourceful, and capable of handling any situation. You'll never find a better man."

Crump glanced at Elmer, and his hostility was abating. "Why, he hasn't even held a steady job for quite a while," he said weakly.

Bud smiled coldly. "He was waiting for the right job. I'm not even sure he'd consider an offer from you."

Crump turned crafty. "I might offer him fifty dollars a month."

Elmer was looking at Bud over Crump's shoulder. Bud shook his head.

Elmer gulped. "Not enough," he said stoutly.

Crump glared at Bud, then turned his head back to Elmer. He appeared desperate, as though he was fearful of losing something valuable. "What would you consider?" he growled.

"I think the going rate for a sheriff is seventy-five dollars a month," Bud said smoothly.

"You keep out of this," Crump yelped.

"That's the figure I had in mind," Elmer said gravely.

"Entirely too much," Crump snapped and started for the door.

"That leaves your town without protection," Bud pointed out.

Crump stopped and turned an agonized face toward the pair. "We'll give it a try," he said helplessly. "But remember this. I can fire you as quickly as I hired you." He stalked on out of the office.

Elmer's face showed his delight. He squeezed Bud's

hand in that big paw. "I can't believe it. I've got a steady job. You've done it again, put me back in your debt."

"It was nothing, Elmer." Bud extracted his hand and flexed his fingers to restore the circulation. "Never let him get an edge on you. Keep ahead of him by doing your job. He's a cranky old bastard. If you think you're in the right, stand up to him. I think unconsciously that fussy old man respects that. You might handle everybody that way until you're firmly established."

"I'll keep it in mind," Elmer said solemnly.

"Will you watch her a little longer for me, Elmer? I've got to get over to the boardinghouse and pick up my things. I won't be long."

"Take as long as you want."

"Better put the cuffs back on her," Bud said grimly. "Don't trust her for a minute."

Elmer chuckled. "I'll do it before you leave. She can't work nothing on me. I'm too old to let a pretty face turn my head."

Bud grinned painfully. He wished he could say the same.

Mrs. Edison saw Bud coming toward the boardinghouse and met him at the door. "Is it true, all the talk I've been hearing?"

"What's that?"

"Did you arrest Lilah for being the head of a horse-stealing ring?"

Bud frowned at her. By now, he supposed everybody in town had heard about Lilah's arrest. "I did. Does it upset you?" She was a woman and would naturally side in with another woman.

She shook her head vigorously. "It does not," she said heatedly. "I never did trust her. She had things going her way too easy."

Bud had miscalculated. Lilah had too much beauty for another woman to be comfortable around her. "I've got to pick up my things," he said. "I'm taking her on the morning stage. She'll face charges in Guthrie."

Bud came back down the steps carrying his warsack, and she was waiting for him. "I just took some freshly-baked apple pies out of the oven. You've got time to try a piece and tell me how it is."

The aroma from the kitchen drifted out to him, and it started the juices in his mouth to running. Come to think of it, he hadn't had much of a breakfast. He looked at the clock on the wall. He had ample time.

He had never eaten better pie. He finished that piece, and she insisted he try another. "Seeing a man happy at her table is about the only pleasure an old woman has."

Bud gave in and finished the second piece. Those and two cups of coffee left him comfortably full. "I've been here over three weeks, Mrs. Edison." Bud pulled out six dollars. "I owe you that for the lodging."

She tried to push the money back, but Bud refused her. "It's more than worth it. Staying here was one of the few pleasures I had in Chandler."

Her face was resigned as she tucked the money away in her bodice. She walked with him to the door. "I've got the feeling you won't be coming back," she said sorrowfully.

"You're probably right. My job's done here. I think I have everything wrapped up. If I ever happen back this way, I'll stop and see you."

"Nothing would delight an old lady more."

He looked back after a few steps. She still stood in the doorway. He touched the brim of his hat. He had made a few friends in Chandler, but not many. He hurried back to the office, and Billy was waiting there.

"When Pa didn't come back, I got worried. He was just telling me about his new job. Say, ain't that great?"

"It sure is," Bud said with feeling. He had something for Billy that would pleasure him no end, but even with the time he had spent with Mrs. Edison it wouldn't happen for almost an hour.

He walked over to Lilah and sat down on the corner of the desk. "Anything you want me to get for you out of your rooms?"

"Do you really mean that?" There was a deceptive softness in her voice that hadn't been there for quite a while. Something crawled across his skin. She's up to something, a little inner voice warned him.

"Bud, I admit I made a mistake," she purred. "But I was born poor, and you don't know what that's like until you've tasted it yourself. I found out I could make a few extra dollars. When I got started, I couldn't stop. For the first time in my life I had money."

Bull, he thought derisively. You had the saloon, and it was doing all right. He waited for her to go on.

"I learned my lesson, Bud," She gave him the full candlepower of her eyes.

He stirred uneasily. "What are you trying to say?"

"Bud, couldn't you just forget about this. I'd make it worthwhile."

Her eyes bored into him, and he squirmed uneasily. She wasn't talking about repayment in dollars. "No," he said stubbornly. "A court has to decide what to do with you."

He caught a flash of lightning in her eyes. That temper was close under the surface.

She drew a deep breath, calming herself. "Bud, I've got a lot of friends here. I can't stand the thought of the shame when you walk me to the stage."

"You should have thought of that earlier," Bud said harshly. She was a devious woman, using every subterfuge at her command. He shook himself and walked away. She was pure poison. There should be a label on her. Old Crump had been wise enough to see it.

A voice said from the doorway, "Is the marshal here?"

Bud recognized the voice. "Right here, Sam. Be out in an instant."

He looked over at the boy. "Billy, come out with me. I've got something to show you."

They walked out together. Billy stared at the horse the livery stable man held, and his eyes grew bigger. He didn't actually know what was going on, but a hope was springing to life.

"Bud, what's this all about?"

Bud handed him a slip of paper. "That's a bill of sale for Lucky. I think it's time to retire old Charley. You treat Lucky real good, hear? He's been a fine horse. You do what you're supposed to do for him, and he'll return it in good service."

Billy's eyes were misting over, and he seemed to have lost his voice. He finally managed to say, "You mean you're giving him to me?"

"Not giving," Bud corrected. "I sold him to you."

"This means you don't plan on coming back?" A sickness spread across his face.

"That's it, Billy."

The boy shook his head. "I'd rather have you stay."

"Things have worked out so that I can't, Billy. I have to take the stage, and I didn't know what to do with Lucky. You take care of him, you hear me?"

Billy looked at Lucky, and his eyes shone like stars. "You know I will," he breathed.

Elmer said from the doorway of the office, "Quarter to ten, Bud. Think you'd better get going. I'm walking down to the depot with you." He didn't say it, but Bud knew what he had in mind. Elmer was coming along in case Bud needed protection. It might be wise to accept his offer. Lilah had said she had a lot of friends in this town. A few of them might be crazy enough to try to make a move.

"Grateful," Bud said and walked past Elmer. He stopped beside the desk and said, "Time to go, Lilah."

He could swear there was pure venom in her eyes, but she didn't try to speak, and he was grateful for that.

Elmer and Bud flanked Lilah on either side. Elmer shook his head at Billy. "You stay here, son. You promised Bud you'd take good care of Lucky. Leaving him now sure wouldn't be a good start."

Billy nodded, his face distressed. His expression showed that he'd had all a kid could stand without breaking into open blubbering.

"I'll see you again one of these days," Bud said softly. He looked back, and Billy stood close to Lucky. Bud felt moistness in his eyes. Damn, he was glad he thought of turning Lucky over to the kid.

Quite a crowd had gathered at the stage depot and a clamor went up at the sight of Lilah. "Don't worry, Lilah," somebody called. "You'll beat it."

Bud's face hardened. He could expect a male audience to take the woman's side, particularly if she was pretty.

"Stay back," he warned. The jeering broke out afresh. Bud was glad to have Elmer and his scatter-gun along.

He walked into the depot, pushing Lilah ahead of him, and bought two tickets. "Do you think the stage is on time?"

The clerk looked at Lilah, and Bud waited for a judgment to cross his face. "It's not due until ten o'clock," the clerk reproved. "It's on time until ten o'clock passes."

Bud sat down with Lilah on one of the hard benches, and Elmer stood near them. It was the longest ten minutes Bud had ever spent.

He heard the rumble of wheels and stood. "Time to go, Lilah."

"You could take these things off," she said, holding out her wrists.

"Not now," he said gravely. "That shows how much I fear you."

He escorted her to the waiting vehicle, shutting his ears to the hooting and catcalls coming from the crowd. When would a crowd learn to respect law and order and not try to hinder it? Bud didn't know. It hadn't happened yet.

He looked up at the driver. "Any passengers?"

The driver nodded. "One. He's inside."

"Ask him to ride up with you." Bud saw the flash of defiance in the driver's eyes and said sternly, "I'm escorting a woman prisoner. It'd be best all around."

The driver looked at Bud's harsh face, then at his badge. He gulped and said weakly, "As you say, sir."

Bud waited until the passenger got out, then helped Lilah into the coach. He took the seat across from her, hoping he wouldn't have to exchange a word with her the entire trip.

The coach hadn't gone two hundred yards when Lilah said tentatively, "Bud—"

He looked frozenly at her. "Yes?"

She looked intently at him, and he had the impression of claws being unsheathed and sharpened.

"Bud, I meant something to you once. It could be that way again."

"Stop it, Lilah."

Her hatred was so great that she couldn't conceal it. "I'll never forget this," she hissed. "One of these days, I'll find a way to pay you back."

Bud hadn't slept much last night, and most of it had been uncomfortable. He was tired, and his head ached. He didn't intend riding all the way to Guthrie listening to her poison.

"Shut up," he roared. The vehemence of his order startled her, and she blinked. His voice lowered a degree. "I mean it, Lilah. I want to get some sleep. Only the judge can do you any good. After I bring you in, it's out of my hands."

"Of all the hardheaded bastards I ever knew—" she started.

"I said, shut up." Bud roared again. The driver could hear that. "I won't tell you a third time."

He sank lower in the seat and pulled his hat over his eyes. From under its brim he could catch a small glimpse of her. The silence grew, and she must have thought he had fallen asleep, for she made no attempt to hide her hatred. He watched the play of emotions on her face. She wasn't a beautiful woman now. He had fallen in love with her, or thought he had. Was he the loser? He didn't know. He had learned caution, but that caution would cost him something. It would make him woman-shy, and *that* would be his loss.